novum pro

AF063130

JAMES K. PAPAY

MR. X:
Assassin
By Desire

novum pro

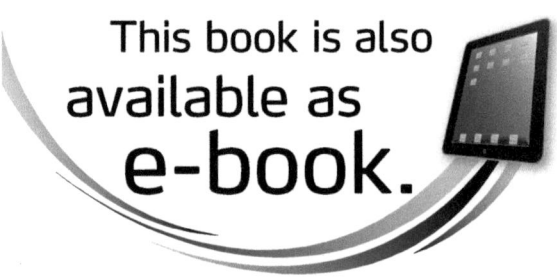

www.novum-publishing.co.uk

All rights of distribution,
including via film, radio, and television,
photomechanical reproduction,
audio storage media, electronic data
storage media, and the reprinting of
portions of text, are reserved

Printed in the European Union on
environmentally friendly, chlorine- and
acid-free paper.

© 2017 novum publishing

ISBN 978-3-99048-547-7
Editing: Louise Darvid
Cover photo:
Artranq | Dreamstime.com
Cover design, layout & typesetting:
novum publishing

www.novum-publishing.co.uk

MR. X

Contents

Introduction 6

Chapter I – The Mutation and Partnership 10

Chapter II – The First Kill and an Assassin is Born 18

Chapter III – Past Recollections 32

Chapter IV – Time for War and
the Body Count Begins 44

Chapter V – First Aid Rendered, Modification
Implemented and Plan Decided 58

Chapter VI – Hit List Finalized and Plan Exercised 70

Chapter VII – Hunting Commences and
MERC Doesn't Hesitate 80

Chapter VIII – Who Is Next? It Could Be You 98

Conclusion 118

Introduction

𝓜𝓻. 𝓧

❖ ❖ ❖

The year is 2030. The beginnings of the 21st century of twenty-five years gone by (2000, 2005, 2015 and 2025), that the human race once knew, is a past memory and is nowhere in comparison to the present day we now live in, to endure for one's survival morning, noon and night.

On 01 January 2029, at 12:00 hours throughout the entire planet earth, it went into simultaneous genocidal chaos for 120 hours. An evil technologist genius, Semi-Human Cyborg by the name, HAKIT took complete control of every country's own military defence systems and turned it against themselves from air, land and sea. Each country's capital was untouched but was helpless and vulnerable to the surmountable strategic invasions from Supreme, DEVIFETAN's ONE GOVERNMENT relentless militia. People everywhere that you come across, that were somehow unfortunate to have lived through the apocalyptic event, know it as to be the "Invasion At High Noon".

ONE GOVERNMENT rule is absolute in each country's capital and the rest of every country's remaining land territory is nothing more than a wasteland of ruins. The elite, wealthy and those selected to be in servitude to these so-called proper people live and work inside the fortified walls encircled around the capitals. All the others not privileged, live and die in the wasteland among the CHAINED, CONVERTED and CRAZIED.

The wasteland outside the capital of Moscow in the Federal Subject of Russia is where I was banished by the ONE GOVERNMENT regime to die but only have survived to live another day. It was discovered by this regime that I was a Spetsgruppa 'A' (Alpha Group or Alfa), a trained and experienced member in special operations, counter-terrorism, hostage rescue and assassination that was assigned to Federal Security Service (FSB) in Moscow.

This deemed me a threat so I was injected with a serum, called 'Exodus Equals Erased' (E^3). It was a 100 % 'concentrate-in-pure-form'; atom sized synthetic living organisms that invaded my bloodstream forced into the jugular veins in my neck.

It was designed to instantaneously manifest through an incubation process, and then aggressively erupt with multiple minute explosions internally to literally vaporize me into nothingness within 120 hours period of time. Instead, these organisms metamorphosed unmeasurable levels of pure oxygen that rushed throughout the systemic circulation transforming both my body and mind in a constant evolution process of cyclic mutation.

After, fifty of my Spetsgruppa comrades and I were injected with the 'Exodus Equals Erased' (E^3) serum against our will, we were shackled together in groups of five by our wrists and ankles, forced to load up into a Mil Mi-26 Russian heavy transport helicopter, that flew to the city of Khimki (21 km) away from the capital of Moscow. We were then shoved out the open rear cargo door of the helicopter as it hovered just above Arena Khimki and we landed in the centre circle of the football field.

Thirty out of fifty of my fellow comrades died on impact when they hit the ground on the football field, and the rest of us sustained broken bones and multiple contusions. As, I lay on the ground I could hear screams of severe pain echoing throughout the arena as I was slowly losing consciousness from the fall I had taken.

When I awoke, I found myself lying in a stranger's bed in an unfamiliar bedroom, with my wounds already attended to, and bandaged and was greeted by a 'Young Easy Sex' (YES) Cyborg Clone named Sindee. She was a slender, curvy female with orange colour skin, large shiny black size eyes and long curly gold hair.

Sindee introduced herself, informed me that this was her one bedroom upstairs flat that I was presently occupying, and explained how she found and rescued me from the cannibal crazed CRAZIED. Then immediately brought me here and treated the wounds I received from being shoved out of a helicopter. She also told me that the others that survived the fall but were badly injured when we landed on to Arena Khimki's football field had been discovered four hours later by these CRAZIED. They dismembered my comrades as they were still alive onsite, and their body parts stockpiled into CRAZIEDs' Black Meat Wagons and taken away.

That day, 14 February 2030, is the day that my life would be changed forever as I was transformed into MR. X; a mutant (30% human and 70% synthetic evolving energy (SEE), an assassin to be feared and talked about as the 'Boogie Man' in every language throughout the wastelands of the world by the CHAINED, CONVERTED and CRAZIED. I was also a mythos within all the ranks of the ONE GOVERNMENT regime.

Also, Sindee a 'Young Easy Sex' (YES) Cyborg Clone, who saved my life from annihilation, would become my assassin's assistant, confidant, dear friend, girlfriend and steadiness to my unpredictable capabilities with reaction to eradicating those that were justifiable due of extermination.

Chapter 1

MR. X - 1

The Mutation and Partnership

The day that I was transformed into MR. X; as a mutant, who was now 30% human and 70% synthetic evolving energy (SEE), Sindee explained to me in detail, what she had witnessed.

She said when she discreetly brought me back to her one bedroom upstairs flat; I was in a semi-conscious state. She took off the blood soaked clothes I was wearing, sponge bathed me from 'head-to-toes', treated every external and internal injury that was found on my body, made me as comfortable as possible and regularly monitored me as I rested in her bed. But on the fifth day under her care, something horrifying began to happen to me and she noticed by the symptoms I was displaying, that I had been infected with the serum, 'Exodus Equals Erased' (E^3).

Knowing that I was a human exposed to the atom sized synthetic living organisms; it was just a question of when the multiple minute explosions internally would literally vaporize me into nothingness. She waited in a corner of the bedroom, hid behind a large aluminium table turned on its side, to shield herself from the debris of my body as they were to cover the whole room. Instead, I went through a mutated transformation process that altered my mental and physical makeup.

After, Sindee told me what had happened to me; I stared at her confused and in disbelief. I asked her if she had a handheld portable mirror that I could use to look at myself. She awkwardly smiled at me, walked over to the large dresser against the far wall of the bedroom to the right-hand side, of where I was sitting up in the bed, reached out and grabbed the handheld portable mirror off the top of it, turned around, came up to me at the right-side of the bed and handed it to me.

𝕸𝖗. 𝒳 - 1

    I slowly lifted the handheld portable mirror up to my face to look into it and was stunned with awe of my appearance. My skin was grey with no hair whatsoever on it throughout the entire outside of my body, except for the coarse wire-like woodland green hair, medium in length, that cover my scalp. My fingernails, lips and tongue were onyx black. My eyes' sclera was crimson red, iris bright green and the pupils resembled those of a snake. I unintentionally let the handheld portable mirror fall out of my left hand that I had gripped it with; it fell on the bedroom wood floor and the mirror glass shattered.

    Sindee slowly approached me where I was sitting up in the bed, gently stroked my coarse wire-like, woodland green hair, sat down on the bed beside me, kissed me on both my cheeks, stood up, took off her clothes, got into the bed naked with me, positioned herself on to my naked body and pulled the covers over the both of us. She orally aroused me with bioengineered stimulant saliva from her mouth on my 'man-tool' as she continued to go down on me and after a while of pleasuring me and herself, she then slithered her chest up to mine, pressed her buttocks tightly into my hips and put it inside her.

    About one hour had passed by before the both of us were finished satisfying one another and she laid her head on my chest, looked up at me with a smile of fulfilment. I looked down at Sindee, as I ran my fingers through her long curly gold hair and asked her if she had any idea what had recently happened to me.

    She told me that I was exposed to a serum called 'Exodus Equals Erased' (E^3), that Chief Biomedical Engineer, Ivan Gott, who works for ONE GOVERNMENT designed and created it as a 100 % 'concentrate-in-pure-form' DNA genetic strand woven into atom sized synthetic living organisms.

    This serum is injected directly into the blood supply through way of a human being's jugular vein. These atom sized synthetic living organisms invade and thrive inside the Haemoglobin (Hb) of the oxygen baseline that transports metalloproteinase in the

Mr. X - 1

red blood cells. Once these atom sized synthetic living organisms are introduced to the bloodstream of a female and/or male human, they immediately manifest through an incubation process, then aggressively erupt multiple minute explosions internally and literally vaporize an individual into nothingness within 120 hours.

Its original intended use was for Semi-Human Clones and 'Young Easy Sex' (YES), Cyborg Clones, such as Sindee, as a DNA implant that allows us to have an unlimited ability to adaption, phenomenal agility, and strength and superior intelligence. Trial experiments of the serum was administered to several thousand homeless and mentally challenged humans throughout the world that produced catastrophic results, hence, 'Exodus Equals Erased' (E^3), was born to eradicate human life when deemed appropriate to eliminate all and any type of threat to ONE GOVERNMENT rule. No human has ever survived a dosage of the serum, 'Exodus Equals Erased' (E^3) within them until now.

I also asked Sindee about the physical change of what has become of me. She commented that what she witnessed first-hand was astonishing, in reference to the conversion process that I had gone through, that could be interpreted as somewhat of a rebirth.

She lifted herself up off my chest, sat up in the bed next to me, stretched her orange colour, smooth, muscular bare legs across my abdomen, looked at me, smiled with a big grin on her face and asked if she could conduct a couple of preliminary tests on me, which would assist her in being able to better answer my question about my physical change. I nodded my head in an up and down motion of approval. So, she lifted her legs up that laid across my abdomen, rolled backward off the other side of the bed, landed on the bottom of her bare feet on the wooden bedroom floor, straightened herself erect and walked naked into the area of the kitchen. She gathered up several items a large stainless steel Butcher knife, Zippo lighter, aluminium frying pan, medium sized white ceramic salad bowl and Rus-

Mr. X - 1

sian 50 kopeks coin, carried them into the bedroom and placed them on the foot of the bed.

The first test was to focus on penetration and puncture of my skin. She grabbed the Butcher knife with her right hand, gripped it tight, instructed me to lift my forearms up in front of me, as if to shield my upper shoulders and throat area and then swung the knife at me in a slashing motion. The sharp cutting edge of the blade went across the meaty portion of my forearms and did not open up the skin, but instead squashed the blade flat.

The second test was to focus on adjustment and regulation of my body temperature. She grabbed the Zippo lighter with her left hand and with the right hand flipped it open, instructed me hold out my hands, palms down in front of me, lit the lighter and ran its flame in a back and forth motion across my fingertips. The flame did not burn and discolour the tips of my fingers, but instead it began to melt the inside case of the lighter.

The third test was to focus on force and power of my strength. She grabbed the aluminium frying pan, gripped it firm with both hands, held it out in front of her at chest height with the bottom facing me, instructed me to make a fist with either hand that I chose and to punch it. My left fist went right through the backside of the pan putting a hole in it.

The fourth test was to focus on description and identification of my thermal vision sensory. She grabbed the medium sized white ceramic salad bowl and Russian 50 kopeks coin, set the salad bowl upside down on the wooden bedroom floor about 5 metres from the foot of the bed I was in, turned her back to me which blocked my view, put the coin in between the palms of her hands, rubbed it vigorously until it began to glow red, tilted up the salad bowl a little bit to place the coin underneath it, stepped off to the side, instructed me to look at it and describe what I saw. My eyes focused on the turned over medium sized white ceramic salad bowl and instantaneously registered a glow-

MR. X - 1

ing circle object underneath it. I told her what was underneath the salad bowl. I said it looked like a coin or token.

Sindee displayed a big smile, giggled aloud, jumped up and down excitedly, clapped her hands together, and confirmed I was correct with the answer I had given to her. Then she suddenly ran and jumped into the bed, dove feet first underneath the covers, leaned into the left side of my exposed upper torso, grabbed hold of both my arms and pulled me on top of her. She reached down between the both of us, grabbed my 'man-tool' with her left hand, started gently jerking it up and down and with her right hand that cupped the top of it, and started softly squeezing it until I was fully erect.

She insisted that she would tell me of her findings, in relation to the couple of preliminary tests, which were conducted on me pertaining to my physical change. But, requested as she playfully giggled at me to have my 'man-tool' placed inside her 'love-box', so we could be joined together as one in unity, while she explained to me exactly what results were produced from the four preliminary tests.

So, I placed my 'man-tool' inside her 'love-box', and she immediately wrapped her legs around the lower area of my back, bit down on the bottom left corner of her lip while smiling and then explained in detail about what each of the four preliminary tests revealed.

The first test in reference to penetration and puncture of the skin revealed that my epidermis is constructed of a graphene exoskeleton structure, almost impenetrable, and made up of carbon atom characteristics. The reason why I have no hair on my body except for my scalp is because the hair follicles serve as ports to stored retractable quills. These quills extend to a full height of 18cm from every follicle, except from the base of the neck to the top of the head, as a defence shielding mechanism on command when enraged or threatened.

After Sindee explained what the first test uncovered in relation to me with penetration and puncture, she suddenly went

MR. X - 1

silent, displayed a pouting look on her face, held up both hands in my face signalling a 10 count total with her thumbs and fingers. I looked down at her with a puzzled expression on my face. She demanded to me that I owe her 10 hard thrusts of placing my 'man-tool' inside her 'love-box', after an explanation of what each preliminary test concluded. I shrugged my shoulders, nodded my head in acknowledgement and gave her the hard thrusts that were required of me.

She tilted her head backwards, tightened the grip of her legs that were wrapped around the lower area of my back, counted aloud to ten and told me to stop. She tilted her head forward, loosened the grip of her legs wrapped around the lower area of my back smiled up at me and explained what the results from the second test were.

Sindee explained the second test in association with adjustment and regulation of my body temperature shown that the pigmentation of my grey skin, onyx black fingernails, lips and tongue were sensors to manipulate at will unlimited variances in fluctuation to distal-to-proximal temperature gradient. The temperature variations are powered by the P300 (P3) wave evoked by the automatic stimulus process of vigilant decision making within my central nervous system.

Then she suddenly went silent, smiled at me, held up both hands in my face signalling a 10 count total with her thumbs and fingers. I acknowledged her demand and continued from where I ceased and she counted aloud to ten and told me to stop.

Sindee explained the third test in correlation with force and power of my strength, demonstrated my ability to fluently generate phenomenal agility and strength that could easily punch through steel 15.24 cm in thickness without doing any internal damage to myself.

Then she suddenly went silent for a third time, smiled at me, held up both hands in my face signalling a 10 count total with her thumbs, and fingers, put one finger and thumb at a time in

Mr. X - 1

her mouth and sucked on each one. I acknowledged her demand once again that was required of me and continued from where I discontinued and she counted aloud to ten and told me to stop.

Sindee explained the fourth test with relationship to description and identification of my thermal vision sensory, can detect microscopic differences in heat signatures as small as 0.01°C temperature with regular clarity. Different materials are absorbed and emitted in different amounts appearing visible to a thermal representation. This ability allows me to form images both during daylight and night-time hours from minute changes in heat between objects. For this reason my eyes' sclera are crimson red, iris bright green and pupil resemble those of a snake.

She once again went silent, smiled at me, but did not hold up both hands in my face signalling a 10 count total with her thumbs and fingers. Instead she loosened the grip of her legs wrapped around my lower area of my back, pressed her buttocks tightly into my hips, retightened the grip of her legs, grabbed a hold of the metal barred headboard frame that was behind her head with both hands and demanded I owed her continuous hard thrusts of placing my 'man-tool' inside her 'love-box' until I was depleted and drained of every last droplet of my internal liquid as she conducted a 'Depletion Extraction Empty Process' (DEEP) to me. I acknowledged her demand that was required of me, continuing where I stopped the last time. She tilted her head backwards, screamed aloud in pleasure to not stop as her whole body shook eagerly to achieve a heightened awakening of sexual stimulus for the first time that was never experienced with male humans that she serviced as an active 'Young Easy Sex' (YES), Cyborg Clone in the escort business.

Chapter II

The First Kill and an Assassin is Born

DEATH DOES NOT DISCRIMINATE
IT ONLY ELIMINATES
DEATH DOES NOT DISCRIMINATE
IT ONLY TERMINATES
THOSE THAT ARE ABETTING

BOTH EYES OPEN
WILL NOW CLOSE

DEATH DOES NOT DISCRIMINATE
IT ONLY ELIMINATES
DEATH DOES NOT DISCRIMINATE
IT ONLY TERMINATES
THOSE THAT ARE BESETTING

A BEATING HEART
WILL NOW STOP

DEATH DOES NOT DISCRIMINATE
IT ONLY ELIMINATES
DEATH DOES NOT DISCRIMINATE
IT ONLY TERMINATES
THOSE THAT ARE CENSURING

A BODY ALIVE
WILL NOW DIE

Mr. X - II

**DEATH DOES NOT DISCRIMINATE
IT ONLY ELIMINATES
DEATH DOES NOT DISCRIMINATE
IT ONLY TERMINATES
THOSE THAT ARE SPECIALIZED
IN ADMINISTERING AGONY, BETRAYAL AND
CONFLICT**

After I had given Sindee the required hard thrusts of placing my 'man-tool' inside her 'love-box' until I was depleted and drained of every last droplet of my internal liquid from her successfully conducted 'Depletion Extraction Empty Process' (DEEP) to me, that produced for her an awakening of sexual stimulus for the first time that she had never experienced as a 'Young Easy Sex' (YES), Cyborg Clone, I noticed the pinkie fingers and toes on her left and right hand and foot were removed.

I was a little bit mystified about the missing pinkie fingers and toes, so I asked her what had happened to them. Sindee looked at me, showing a smile of uneasiness, kissed me on the forehead and told me how they disappeared.

She was once an active 'Young Easy Sex' (YES), Cyborg Clone created by her inventor Victor Young, who began to manufacture 'Young Easy Sex' (YES), Cyborg Clones, both male and female in gender, in the year 2020, to monopolize the global supply and demand in the escort business and sex industry.

She and two other female YES, Cyborg Clone siblings were assigned to operate in Hong Kong, China. While being over there for about one week, she was called out to provide services to a male client, who was from the city of Prague in the Czech Republic, visiting the city of Hong Kong for a week long round of business meetings.

Victor Young's Asian Escort Agency immediately accommodated his request of services needed because he was a well-known wealthy Media Mogul throughout Eastern Europe and

Asia, with a net worth on the World Stock Exchange of 3 billion euros (3,148,950,000 US Dollars or 2,135,678,003 British Pound Sterling). He was educated with a PhD in Global Business and Marketing, 35 years old and a handsome bachelor with consistent accomplishments, overwhelming credentials and star studded portfolio, but he also came across as a genuine person with a kind heart.

After their first time together had concluded, the cost to him was 13,233.37 euros (15,000.00 US Dollars or 9,722.58 British Pound Sterling) for three hours of her company, but he insisted that he would like her to return tomorrow and every day afterwards, until the week long business meetings were finished. She advised him that her employer would need to be notified by him prior to any arrangements being worked out to meet his request. He promptly agreed and informed her that he would contact her employer, first thing the next day, in the early morning sometime before he had to attend the first business meeting on his agenda.

The next day sometime in the afternoon, she received a text message on the company mobile phone issued to her, verified an authorization of services for a client along with the client's details. The client information was the businessman, who paid for her services the evening before. She replied back with a confirmation text message and smiled because her last encounter with this specific individual was an enjoyable one, not like most of the other nasty perverted clients she had to deal with in the escort business.

The four days he spent with her cost him 24,2107.68 euros (27,428.57 USD or 17,7876.96 BPS) that her employer awarded him a 1.75 division discount on the original total price which was 42,346.79 euros (48,000.00 USD or 31,112.26 BPS).

She affirmed that those days were unforgettable, not because of the services she was able to provide to him, but because for the first time, she experienced what it could have possibly felt like to be almost human. Through his eyes, he did not see her as a YES, Cyborg Clone designed to pleasure and satisfy the human race of adult males and females, but as if she was a real-life female human being.

But the memorable time she spent with him ended horribly the last night they were together before he had to leave Hong Kong and return home to Prague. It was exactly at midnight when she received a text message on the company mobile phone issued to her. The text message sent to the mobile phone was from Victor Young's Asian Escort Agency Area Manager based in Hong Kong.

He informed her that a 'Termination Order Protocol' (TOP) on the client she was presently with was authorized by the directive of Victor Young. A minute elapsed after the initial text message was sent to the company mobile phone. Then she received a second text message that instructed her to leave the hotel room within 10 minutes and to put one of the hotel room door access swipe cards on top of the outside door ledge in the hallway that led to the client's room. The reason for the instructions given was that a YES, Cyborg Breeder Clone and YES, Cyborg Collector Clone was en route to carry out a 'Termination Order Protocol' (TOP) on the client. Momentarily after she read the second text message that instructed her of what to do, she received a third and final message which demanded an acknowledgement.

She stared motionless at the last text message from the Agency Area Manager that she received, for several seconds that seemed to be for an eternity.

Suddenly, without comprehension to why, she ran over to the side of the bed where the client lay asleep and frantically shook him with a strong force to wake up. He opened his eyes with a dazed look on his face to why she had rudely awoken him from a deep sleep so late at night. She insisted the need for him to quickly get out of the bed, change into clothes and come with her at an instant.

As he sat up in the bed, pulled the covers off of himself to stand up, the male, Cyborg Collector Clone, flung open the

MR. X - 11

hotel room door to the VIP Presidential Suite room, rushed in toward them and executed a right hook across the left cheekbone area of the startled wealthy Media Mogul, that instantly knocked him unconscious, as he fell backwards on to the bed. The female, Cyborg Breeder Clone entered the room, slipped out of her pink latex body suit, walked over to side of the bed where he laid unconscious, bent over and orally forced him into an erected state. As soon as he remained erect, she jumped on top of him, forced himself inside her and began the 'Vaginal-Vacuum Immobilization Participant Extraction Resources' (V-VIPER) that drew out every ounce of bodily fluid and semen that he contained.

She watched horrified at the atrocities performed on the wealthy Media Mogul, as he laid paralyzed in severe agony on the bed cringing as blood flowed out of the corners of his mouth, down the sides of his face and back of his neck, that stained the bed sheet underneath his head.

The male, Cyborg Collector Clone walked up to her, stepped in her face, accused her of attempting to assist a client to escape, called her a worthless excuse for a functioning sex toy and backhanded her across her face. The backhand given to her lifted her up off her feet which caused her to hit her head off the metal frame of the large wall mounted mirror that knocked her out cold.

When she woke up she lay naked among trash in a large industrial metal disposal box at Hong Kong Park on 19 Cotton Tree Drive, 800 metres from the Conrad Hong Kong Hotel on One Pacific Place, Pacific Place, 88 Queensway. That is when she noticed that her pinkie fingers and toes on her left and right hand and foot were removed, which signified to everyone in the escort business and sex industry that she was indefinitely deactivated to provide services of any kind. It was also a warning, that if any business owner decided to disobey the 'Indefinite Deactivate Order' (IDO) pertaining to her, they would be permanently replaced and all their assets would be seized by Victor Young.

Mr. X - II

All her belongings, such as company issued mobile phone and gold and silver ATM-Debit-Credit cards, Victor Young Global Agency Licenses, and YES Cyborg Clone Registration Identification Card were confiscated and destroyed.

I showed a look of sympathy toward Sindee, shook my head in disgust, wrapped my arms around her upper torso, pulled her in close to me and gave her a firm hug. Afterwards, I felt myself become enraged as I thought about the two individuals, Ivan Gott and Victor Young.

I asked Sindee where I could locate this Chief Biomedical Engineer, Ivan Gott, who works for ONE GOVERNMENT that designed and created the serum called 'Exodus Equals Erased' (E^3), a 100 % 'concentrate-in-pure-form' DNA genetic strand woven into atom sized synthetic living organisms, that he injected me and fifty of my Spetsgruppa comrades against our will? Sindee looked mesmerized at me for a moment, and then snapped out of the brief daze she was in and hesitantly answered my question to the possible whereabouts of ONE GOVERNMENT's Chief Biomedical Engineer, Ivan Gott.

She said that Ivan Gott resides at the Stenbock House that is set on a limestone hill called Toompea in the capital city of Tallinn that used to be where The Government of the Republic of Estonia was located. Ivan Gott also works out of the once National Institute of Chemical Physics and Biophysics in Estonia, Tallinn at the address Akadeemia tee 23. ONE GOVERNMENT's Supreme, DEVIFETAN awarded him the country of Estonia to own, and supplied him with 15,000 ONE GOVERNMENT Security Force Personnel and 3,000 ONE GOVERNMENT Frontline Expendable Suicide Soldiers (OGFESS) to ensure ONE GOVERNMENT absolute rule within that country's capital city.

After, Sindee provided me with the useful information in reference to Ivan Gott, she looked at me 'wide-eyed' with eagerness and asked me why I was interested in Ivan Gott's whereabouts? I smirked with a 'bone chilling', 'skin rippling', vicious glare and declared to her that I was going to kill the motherfucker!

As I disclosed my decision pertaining to assassinating ONE GOVERNMENT's Chief Biomedical Engineer, Ivan Gott , Sindee cautiously backed up away from where I stood with a look of shock emphasized on her face. I asked her if she was alright. She pointed at me with one of her orange colour long forefingers, informed me that my quills had extended to a full height of 18cm from every follicle on my body except from the base of the neck to the top of the head, at the tips of them were glowing bright florescent green and secreting a sparkling yellow liquid, and my coarse wire-like woodland green hair, medium in length, that covered my scalp also was glowing and generating a low pitch buzzing noise.

I reassured Sindee that I had no intention to harm her in any way, as the quills retracted into each follicle that they extended from throughout my body, and the coarse wire-like woodland green hair, medium in length, that covered my scalp also stopped glowing and generating the low pitch buzzing noise it had done previously.

She displayed a big elated smile, repeatedly giggled joyfully, skipped merrily toward me and jumped playfully into my arms. I outstretched my arms and caught her as she descended upon me. I cradled her close against me, looked down at her and asked her where I could acquire a sniper rifle and some pistols. She looked up at me and frowned with worry written all over her face.

Sindee apprehensively informed me that we would have to see the ringleader of the CHAINED sect named Shackle, who is a lewd psychopath and treacherous individual to do business of any kind with whatsoever.

I set Sindee down on the left side of the bed, from being cradled in my arms and made certain nothing bad would happen to either of us when we visit the ringleader of the CHAINED sect named Shackle to do business. She jumped to her feet, stood on

MR. X - 11

her tippy toes, reached up, kissed me on my forehead, smiled at me with delight and demanded then that we both hurry up and get dressed to go see him.

The both of us got dressed, left Sindee's one bedroom upstairs flat and headed to Khimki City Hall where Shackle was headquartered to meet with him. As Sindee and I drew near to the front driveway that led to the entrance of the building, we were stopped and questioned 50 metres away from it by three CHAINED-Security Roving Foot Patrol Clansmen (C-SRFP-C) each armed with a Vityaz-SN, semi-automatic and fully automatic, submachine guns. The premises were encircled 360 degrees with concrete block walls, 7 metres high x 4 metres wide x 3 metres thick, that conveyed the impression of an impenetrable fortress.

Sindee explained to the CHAINED-Security Roving Foot Patrol Clansman (C-SRFP-C), who initially questioned our intentions for hanging around too close to the CHAINED Headquarters, that we were here to meet with Shackle about a matter of interest. The three C-SRFP-C stared silently at us for a brief moment and then hysterically laughed aloud. They raised their Vityaz-SN, semi-automatic and fully automatic, submachine guns, pointed them at us and the one who seemed to be in charge of the other two sarcastically inquired if we were prepared to be machine gunned to death.

Sindee raised her outstretched arms to chest level with the palms of her hands facing out toward them and pleaded for them not to shoot, but to give Shackle a call to let him know that she was here to see him. The one that was the leader of the group, smiled with a sly look on his face, pulled out the walkie-talkie phone that was in the left breast pocket of his dirty faded black leather jacket and called Shackle, while the other two C-SRFP-C continued to still have their Vityaz-SN, semi-automatic and fully automatic, submachine guns pointed at us as the phone call was being made to inform Shackle who was outside the walls of the CHAINED Headquarters to see him.

MR. X - II

The leader of the group with the walkie-talkie phone held it up to his right ear, intently listening to what instructions were given to him by Shackle. When Shackle was finished with what he had to say, the leader of the group acknowledged by saying "Yes, Boss", ended the call and put the walkie-talkie phone back into the left breast pocket of his dirty faded black leather jacket. He looked at Sindee and I with a 'dead stare' then led us through the front grey metal reinforced gate into the impenetrable fortress. We walked up the pathway to the entrance of the CHAINED Headquarters building with the leader of the group out in front of us and the other two CHAINED-Security Roving Foot Patrol Clansmen (C-SRFP-C) following right behind with their submachine guns pointed at our backside. As soon as we reached the front entrance to the CHAINED Headquarters building we were met by two CHAINED-Security Building Patrol Clansmen (C-SBP-C) standing guard at the front doors into the building.

The leader of the group of CHAINED-Security Roving Foot Patrol Clansmen (C-SRFP-C) informed the two CHAINED-Security Building Patrol Clansmen (C-SBP-C) that Sindee and I were here to see Shackle. They acknowledged and one of the CHAINED-Security Building Patrol Clansmen (C-SBP-C) commanded us to follow him inside the building. He escorted us along through a large black and white checker marble foyer and into a huge open room where in the middle of it a giant muscular man in stature sat in a red upholstered throne-like chair. It was Shackle, the ringleader of the CHAINED sect. I estimated his height to be about 2.25 metres and weight 227 kilograms. He had long intense auburn colour hair braided in a ponytail laid over his left shoulder that reached the bottom of his chest and a thick rectangular shaped beard the same colour that touched flush at the base of his neck. He had a shiny chunky gold chain link necklace with a miniature functioning brass hourglass pendant affixed to it around his neck. The colour of his skin was a Jaundice yellow pigment and protruding the full length of both forearms, from wrists to elbows; completely around them were surgically implanted 5 centimetres high black fishhook like spikes. He wore a charcoal colour sleeveless chain mesh vest, dirty faded black leather biker trousers and scuffed up black Doc Martens boots.

Shackle sat egotistically proud on his throne in the huge open room he named the Hall Of Faces surrounded by four personally assigned CHAINED-Security Bodyguard Clansmen (C-SB-C) hand-picked by himself. On his right-hand side wrapped around his right hand, he gripped three separate long metal chains. At the other end of the chains were female YES, Cyborg Breeder Clones with metal collars around their necks performing 'Vaginal-Vacuum Immobilization Participant Extraction Resources' (V-VIPER) to a naked man. His eyes were opened wide in terror, as he lay paralyzed on his back in severe agony on the concrete floor vigorously cringing. Blood flowed out of the corners of his mouth, down the sides of his face and back of his neck underneath his head as every ounce of bodily fluid and semen was forcibly extracted from his body. On Shackle's left-hand-side he held tightly in his left hand a 91 centimetres long electric shock baton. He periodically poked the other three naked men huddled together, shaking in fear, with their backs turned toward him at the far end of the 1.8 metres high x 3.6 metres wide metal bird cage prison that they were detained in.

Shackle looked at Sindee and I with a malicious glare and asked us if we knew how to get even with someone who has tried to 'fuck-you-over'. The both of us remained silent and exhibited blank stares. He laughed aloud turned his head to the right, rattled the three long metal chains gripped in his right hand and told us that you literally 'fuck-em-right-back'. The four personally assigned CHAINED-Security Bodyguard Clansmen (C-SB-C) that he 'hand-picked' laughed along with him. I felt rage rush throughout every vein within my body.

Shackle turned his attention back to us again and inquired of Sindee what we were in need of from him. Sindee began to disclose our purpose for visiting him, when suddenly he interrupted her and demanded that she pleasure him as she had done in the past when she was in dire need of something and afterwards he would listen to her request. He leaned the long electric shock baton against the left armrest of the red upholstered throne-like chair. Then he stood up, with his freehand pulled down the zipper on the dirty faded black leather biker trousers, reached inside them, pulled out his 'man-tool' and sat back down on the seat of the throne-like chair. I felt the rage already inside my veins within my body start to boil my blood.

Sindee shivered with dreadfulness as Shackle insisted she come to him pronto. She slowly turned her head to look at me in anguish before regrettably going over to where Shackle sat in his throne. Before she made one step in the direction of Shackle, I grabbed her left wrist with my right hand and pulled her behind me.

I felt the rage inside me peak to its highest point I had ever experienced in my 'life-to-date' and then without hesitation 'Filter Reasoning Flat-Lined' (FRFL) activated, that consumed every human emotion at one time, in which everything became quiet inside of me and outside my body in relation to my surroundings. My left hand to arm to elbow transformed into a cylindrical pointed spike. I leaped forward toward Shackle where he sat on his throne, thrust the cylindrical pointed spike up under his chin, piercing him through his mouth, between his eyes and out of the top of his skull. I pulled back my transformed cylindrical pointed spike that impaled Shackle completely through the head. It was covered in blood with debris of some skin and pieces of brain matter. He fell forward out of his throne and face first on to the concrete floor where he began to bleed out from being speared through the head. Shackle's CHAINED-Security Bodyguard Clansmen (C-SB-C) stood motionless for an instant in awe to what had just happened to their ringleader of the CHAINED sect. But once the initial shock had diminished, they unanimously attempted to pull, raise and shoot me with their MP-443 Grach, double-action, short-recoil semi-automatic pistols, but I had already extended my quills to their full height of 18cm from every follicle as a precautionary measure defence shielding mechanism on command when enraged or threatened. Before any one or all of the four CHAINED-Security Bodyguard Clansmen (C-SB-C) could squeeze a round off at me, I discharged four individual quills intended for each one of them that blew through the centre of their chests and out their backs. All four of the CHAINED-Security Bodyguard Clansmen (C-SB-C) dropped dead where they stood.

Then I turned around, looked at Sindee and put my right hand out to her as a sign that it was time to leave the Hall Of Faces to return to her one bedroom upstairs flat so we could regroup, and figure out what plan next would be deemed appropriate to proceed with.

Sindee stood frozen as she stared at me astonished at what had just happened. I called out her name three times before she snapped out of whatever trance she was in. She reached out with her left and grabbed my right hand as she shook back and forth her long curly gold hair in amazement to what she had witnessed pertaining to me with how quickly I eliminated Shackle and his personally assigned four CHAINED-Security Bodyguard Clansmen (C-SB-C).

We departed the huge open room named the Hall Of Faces and headed toward the large black and white checked marble foyer. Sindee looked up at me as we were about to enter the foyer and asked me if I knew what I had just done. I affirmed that I had exterminated a worthless waste of a so-called human being, who was vile through-and-through and the supposed ringleader of the deranged CHAINED sect. She agreed without scepticism with what I expressed to her, but informed me that I did not correctly answer the question she requested from me. I explained to her that it was what I thought she had implied with regards to assassinating Shackle.

Sindee enlightened me of what she had witnessed pertinent to executing flawlessly 'Filter Reasoning Flat-Lined' (FRFL), which she had never known to be performed by any human being, type of Cyborg or Cyborg Clone . She only knew of 'Conceived Artificial Life Forms' (CALFS) that had been genetically programed with the ability to be 'CALM, COLLECTIVE, COOL and FOCUSED' (C^3-F), capable of such an act of precision with the consumption of every human emotion at one time when in the 'Eye Of This Storm' per se. Also, she revealed it was rumoured but not proven that DEVIFETAN is the first original 'Conceived Artificial Life Form' (CALF) and that all the others after him were hunted down and murdered by his 'Order Uncover Threats' (OUT), carried out six months before January 1 2029, simultaneous invasion throughout the entire planet earth.

Chapter III

Mr. X - III

Past Recollections

Sindee and I quietly proceeded down the large black and white checked marble foyer and kept close to each side of its walls to be sure not to produce silhouettes that would draw the attention of the two CHAINED-Security Building Patrol Clansmen (C-SBP-C) that stood guard at the front doors into the building. When we were almost one metre from the large solid oak wood and round glass double entry door, I looked across over to her, put my right forefinger to my lips as a hint to be silent, and to stay put as I moved forward to the door. She smiled and acknowledged my request by exhibiting two thumbs up with both her hands in the air for me to see.

I then continued to move the remaining one metre of distance until I reached the large solid oak wood and round glass double entry door. I discreetly peeked out of the edge of the left half round window pane to where the C-SBP-C guards stood positioned outside the double entry door. Both of them were posted at the bottom concrete step of the three concrete steps that led to the front doors into the building. I manufactured a shallow pitch annoying squeal of a strange sound only intense enough for the both of them to hear and become curious to investigate what it could be. I effectively performed this sound at five thirty second intervals before the both of them decided to enter the building to look into where in the noise had been coming from.

As soon as the two C-SBP-C guards entered into the large black and white checked marble foyer, and closed the huge solid oak wood and round glass double entry door behind them, I sprung out from their blindside. When they turned their heads to the right over their shoulders I thrust my left and right forearms

Mr. X - III

with the quills extended to full height of 18cm from every follicle into their necks that penetrated through and out the other ends. I then retracted the quills that were embedded into their necks and severed their heads from their bodies. The two C-SBP-C guards' heads and bodies dropped hard onto the glossy white floor of the black and white checked marble foyer.

I signalled for Sindee to come to my location where I stood over the decapitated bodies. She quickly arrived to my position and I told her to help me gather up the C-SBP-C guards' Vityaz-SN, semi-automatic and fully automatic submachine guns, MP-443 Grach, double-action, short-recoil semi-automatic pistols, ammo shoulder harnesses and vests with complete basic combat issued load, walkie-talkie phones and ZOOM 20-180x100, HDMI night vision binoculars. We bent down over the deceased guards' bodies and collected the items that I instructed her to take with us.

I looked over at Sindee as she was going about her assigned task. I pointed to the pistol and submachine gun she had placed on the body she was leaned over and asked her if she knew how to use them. She stopped what she was doing, picked up the MP-443 Grach, double-action, short-recoil semi-automatic pistol with her left hand, scanned it with her large shiny black eyes, set it back down where she picked it up, grabbed the Vityaz-SN, semi-automatic and fully automatic, submachine gun with both her hands, also scanned it with her large shiny black eyes and nodded her head with confirmation that she did now. I smiled, shook my head back and forth in admiration and went to finishing up what I had been doing.

After, Sindee and I obtained the items I asked to get and were prepared to exit the building, she forewarned me that she was not programed for 'Assignation Conformation Termination' (ACT) or killing a human being only to incapacitate with self-defence combative techniques in response to clients who attempted to harm her in any way before, during or after services were ren-

M.?. X - III

dered. I advised her that she better determinedly override the program for non-lethal, self-defence combative techniques because we might have to 'shoot-to-kill' our way outside the walls of the CHAINED Headquarters impenetrable fortress.

Sindee and I swiftly exited the CHAINED Headquarters building then walked down the pathway away from the entrance of it and toward the front grey metal reinforced gate of the impenetrable fortress. We were about 150 metres from the front grey metal reinforced gate, when we observed the three CHAINED-Security Roving Foot Patrol Clansmen (C-SRFP-C) sat in a black duct taped up in multiple areas, long dark brown cloth material worn torn 3-passenger van bench seat with their backs to us. I looked at Sindee and with both my hands made a 'break-of-the neck' sign. She looked at me, showed a frown, a smile and then nodded her head in confirmation of what needed to be done to the three CHAINED-Security Roving Foot Patrol Clansmen (C-SRFP-C) in order to leave outside the walls of the CHAINED Headquarters through the front grey metal reinforced gate.

The both of us moved quickly and tacitly toward their location. When we were about five metres from being 'right-on-top' of them I noticed that the two CHAINED-Security Roving Foot Patrol Clansmen (C-SRFP-C) sitting on the left and right ends of the 3-passenger van bench seat were asleep and the one guard in the middle between was awake, with a ZOOM 20-180x100, HDMI night vision binoculars held up to his eyes, as he seemed to be surveying for movement out in the distance. I simultaneously grabbed his chin and back of the head with my hands, forcibly twisted his head around 180 degrees to back portion in between his shoulder blades, breaking his neck. Then Sindee and I in unison did the same thing to the other two that sat on the left and right ends of 3-passenger van bench seat that were awoke by the commotion.

Once again, I told Sindee to help me gather up the C-SRFP-C guards' Vityaz-SN, semi-automatic and fully automatic, subma-

MR. X - III

chine guns, ammo vests with complete basic combat issued load, walkie-talkie phone and ZOOM 20-180x100, HDMI night vision binoculars.

Sindee and I attained the items from the C-SRFP-C guards, opened the front grey metal reinforced gate to the CHAINED Headquarters impenetrable fortress, dashed outside its walls away from it and speedily were en route back to her one bedroom upstairs flat before sunset when the CRAZIED mobs would come out.

When we arrived back at Sindee's one bedroom upstairs flat and entered inside, I went straight into her kitchen. I sat down on one of the slender metal framed chairs with dingy off yellow upholstery, laid my forehead on top of the edge of the small-in-width chocolate brown colour wooden kitchen table and closed my eyes. I called out to Sindee if she had anything appetizing to eat in her refrigerator. She jubilantly skipped into kitchen and told me that she would be delighted to heat up a plate of Vareniki (pierogies, filled with potatoes, cheese, mushrooms and squirrel mincemeat) that she had made a day ago that were leftover in the refrigerator. I expressed my gratitude for obliging to feed me because I was famished.

Sindee lightly rubbed my right shoulder with her right hand as she walked by me into the kitchen on her way to the refrigerator to take out the plate of Vareniki that she intended to heat up on the small off white colour vintage looking wood burning stove for me to feast upon. She joyously mentioned repeatedly to me how impressed she had been with herself in performing an independent override to the program for non-lethal, self-defence combative techniques. As she chattered on about the day of earlier events that took place between her and I at the CHAINED Headquarters that pertained to Shackle the ringleader of the CHAINED sect, his four CHAINED-Security Bodyguard Clansmen, the two CHAINED-Security Building Patrol Clansmen and three CHAINED-Security Roving Foot Patrol Clansmen, she abruptly changed the topic to inquire about my life history.

Mr. X - III

I lifted my forehead up off the top of the edge of the narrow chocolate brown colour wooden kitchen table, opened my eyes and asked her what she would like to know about me. She questioned me about the background of my childhood, information about my parents and what determined my decision to enlist in the Russian military to become a Spetsgruppa 'A' (Alpha Group or Alfa), trained and experienced member in special operations, counter-terrorism, hostage rescue and, assassination assigned to the Federal Security Service (FSB) in Moscow. I rubbed both of my eyes with my hands, snickered in a low voice to myself and asked her if she was positive she undoubtedly wanted to listen to my life story. Sindee made it certain beyond a doubt she was interested to hear what I had to say. I shrugged both my shoulders and started from the beginning to divulge the information she desired of me.

I was born towards the end of the hottest summer month in the city of Novosibirsk located in the region of Siberia, Russia in the year of 1999. My mother was a caring, loving and nurturing parent and a devout GOD fearing religious woman, before she agreed to marry my father and shortly afterwards became pregnant with me at the age of 21 years old. She worked for a telecommunications and Internet service provider company in Siberia called Sibirtelecom. My father worked for a company called Siberian Anthracite which is the largest coal company in Novosibirsk region. They were married for 13 years (1998 through 2011) until they divorced due to my father's perpetual addiction to alcohol, illegal drugs and the elicit enticement of prostitutes.

I was just an innocent child when I was forced to observe a grisly world, helpless and vulnerable to the ugliness, of what I would be involuntarily exposed to experience by my father firsthand for years to come. My mother did everything within her power to protect me from my father's evil ways. He was endless in dramatic fashion of his abuse toward me verbally with every opportunity available to him. It was as if his sole mission in life was to erase any confidence I had within myself, by always making sure he belittled me. He always had this favourite hurtful saying that he would imply of me; *"IF YOUR BRAIN WAS MADE OF GUN POWDER, YOU COULD NOT DO ANY DAMAGE IF YOUR LIFE DEPENDED ON IT!"*

I grudgingly became his sacrificial offering, to vindictiveness bred in corruption hidden from the naked eye of the entire human race. My father's intentions toward me were far from obtaining genuine care, love, mentorship and nurture from him in reference to a father/son relationship. He instead attained a heightened enjoyment by inflicting constant mental horror, in the first degree every waking day, which was specifically meant for me. Those 13 years resembled an eternity of purgatory that seemed to have no distant closure for the future. It was not until one echoing day when my mother directed me to sit down on the turquoise colour imitation leather upholstered love sofa in the sitting room, because she had something of valued importance to explain to me about my father. She disclosed to me without exhibiting any disrespect toward him even though he was more than deserving of it, because of how he acted with regard to my mother and I, that they were getting a divorce.

From then on, until I turned 18 years old and graduated my senior year from grade 11, my father did everything available within measure to fill mine and my mother's lives with endless torment. During the first month of the summer season in the year of 2017, I enlisted in the Army of the Russian Federation and originally became a Soldier in the Mechanized Infantry until 3 years later when I was presented the opportunity to be a Russian Airborne Paratrooper (VDV) in the Light Infantry and then 5 years after that was successfully selected to be a Spetsgruppa 'A' to the present, before ONE GOVERNMENT's domination over the entire Planet Earth.

When my parents separated and eventually divorced in October 2012, I was 13 years old. My mother promptly went back to

MR. X - III

work for her previous employer Sibirtelecom who became part of Rostelecom, one of Russia's leading long-distance telephone providers, a year prior in April 2011. She worked for the company fulltime until I completed my accelerated combat training programme and was afterwards assigned to a Mechanized Infantry Unit at which time she happened to live with me permanently at my invitation, because I was a career soldier that never married or had any children of my own with any woman.

A one-time neighbourhood friend of mine named Tatyana that I grew up and attended school with contacted me to mention that she had seen in the NOVAYA SIBIR newspaper that on New Year's Day 2021, my father passed away in a men's toilet stall at a local nightclub, called the Rock City from a drug overdose. I was not surprised one bit nor 'gave two shits' to what I had heard of the news about my father from her.

When I had finished a summarized version of the past to the present background of my life that covered the essential segments with relation to me, I saw Sindee's face overcome with compassion. She beamed with affection for what she had heard that I opened up to her about me. She walked over to me with the plate of Vareniki that she heated up on the small off white colour vintage looking wood burning stove to feast upon, placed it in front of me on the narrow chocolate brown colour wooden kitchen table, bent down with her arms opened wide and gave me a big warm-hearted hug as I sat on a slender metal framed chair with dingy off yellow upholstery.

After she hugged me for about a minute, she stood up, pulled the other slender metal framed chair with dingy off yellow upholstery away from the narrow chocolate brown colour wooden kitchen table and sat down on it.

Sindee then turned her head in my direction to look at me as she began to speak aloud about herself with distaste in her voice that referred to her experience of being activated to life. Ivan Gott, Victor Young and his twin sibling, Vivian Young indulged themselves in sexual gratification with every YES Cyborg Clone, both male and female by taking them for a 'trial test run' of limitless perversion at Victor Young's annual 'Initiation Sex Orgy' (ISO). It was a twenty-four hour event that began at 1200 hours and ended at 1200 hours the following day. Victor Young and his long-time business partner and best friend, Ivan Gott delighted themselves with 'Sample Sex' (SS) of all the female YES Cyborg Clones, in either 'one-on-one', 'tag-team' and/or 'five-to-ten; assembly-line'. Vivian Young pleasured herself with 'Sample Sex' (SS) of the male YES Cyborg Clones, in either 'one-on-one', 'two-to-one', 'three-to-one' or 'nine-twelve-thirteen group sessions'. This anomaly was considered a 'rite of passage' for all the male and female YES Cyborg Clones before they were commissioned to service in the escort business or sex industry.

It was rumoured that Vivian Young was 80% artificial and 20% natural-original human because of the routine cosmetic surgeries performed for her by her brother, because of her addictive obsession to what a perfect example of a female human specimen should've been like.

I exhaled in repugnance at how badly contorted this world had become, when wretched men and women alike situated themselves 'at-the-bottom-of-the-barrel', to drown in the poisonous waste of everything once considered obviously wrong.

MR. X - III

MR. X's Intimate Thoughts:

HAVE YOU EVER HEARD THE SAYING?
NEVER JUDGE A BOOK
BY ITS COVER
BECAUSE IT CAN BE DECEIVING

MISCONCEPTION OF ME-I AM NOT-WHAT I SEEM
TO BE
MISCONCEPTION OF ME-I AM A GIVER-NOT A VICTIM

YOU FORSEE KNOWING EVERYTHING ABOUT ME
THE TRUTH IS
YOU HAVE NOT A CLUE
OF WHO I AM

MISCONCEPTION OF ME-I AM NOT-WHAT I SEEM
TO BE
MISCONCEPTION OF ME-I AM A GIVER-NOT A VICTIM

WHAT YOU THINK YOU KNOW
THAT RELATES TO ME
OF WHAT I AM ALL ABOUT
IS NOT WHAT IT SEEMS TO BE

MISCONCEPTION OF ME-I AM NOT-WHAT I SEEM
TO BE
MISCONCEPTION OF ME-I AM A GIVER-NOT
A RECEIVER

MR. X's Intimate Thoughts:

HEAR NO MORE
THE SOUNDS OF THUNDER
WITH VOICES OF HORROR

SEE NO MORE
THIS WORLD OF MADNESS
WITH FACES OF SADNESS

SPEAK NO MORE
THE NONSENSE OF REASON
WITH WORDS OF TREASON

HEAR NO MORE-SEE NO MORE-SPEAK NO MORE
TO ME-TO ME-TO ME
BECAUSE NOW I AM FOREVER FREE

HEAR NO MORE
THE CONSTANT OF WHISPERS
WITH CONNOTATIONS OF WICKEDNESS

SEE NO MORE
THE GHOSTS OF YESTERDAYS
WITH EYES OF SHAME

SPEAK NO MORE
THE LANGUAGE OF VICTORY
WITH SUGGESTION OF MISGIVINGS
HEAR NO MORE-SEE NO MORE-SPEAK NO MORE
TO ME-TO ME-TO ME
BECAUSE NOW I AM FOREVER FREE

MR. X - III

MR. X's Intimate Thoughts:

YOU FEEL JOY
YOU FEEL LOVE
BUT I PRAY FOR NONE

BECAUSE I HAVE BECOME
THE MAN OF DARKNESS ...

YOU NEED COMFORT
YOU NEED WARMTH
BUT I WISH FOR NONE

BECAUSE I HAVE BECOME
THE MAN OF DARKNESS ...

I AM BELIEVED
TO OWN A COLD HEART
WITH AN EMPTY SOUL

BECAUSE I HAVE BECOME
THE MAN OF DARKNESS ...

I AM PERCEIVED
AS BEING NAMELESS
IN A CROWD OF FACES

BECAUSE I HAVE BECOME
THE MAN OF DARKNESS ...

Chapter IV

Mr. X - IV

Time for War and the Body Count Begins

I gobbled up every bit of that Vareniki on the plate that Sindee heated up for me to eat and placed in front of me on the kitchen table. After I had finished off the meal prepared for me, Sindee handed me an ice cold 5.2% Alcohol By Volume (ABV) bottle of Permskoye Gubernskoye (pale lager beer) to supress my thirstiness after the large plate of food I had devoured. I grabbed the bottle of beer from out of her hand that she provided to me, looked delighted to be given it and told her thank you for everything.

Sindee sat across the narrow chocolate brown colour wooden kitchen table from me, on the other slender metal framed chair with dingy off yellow upholstery, looking pleased and inquired what I planned to do next. I set the bottle of Permskoye Gubernskoye down on the kitchen table after had taken five consecutive gulps, and announced with a serious tone in my voice, that the moment had arrived to forge a formidable statement of panic and bloodshed, to those who are overdue for what they have done.

MR. X - IV

MR. X's Intimate Thoughts:

CAN YOU SEE IT?
AN IMPRESSIVE GREAT THRONE
FORGED OUT OF GOLD

CAN YOU SEE HIM?
SEATED IN THIS THRONE
THE LEGITIMATE GOD UNIMPOSED

PLANET EARTH AND ITS SKY
ARE HIS VIEW FROM ABOVE
OVERSEEING GROSS ACTS OF OBSCENITY

THE DEAD WILL BE JUDGED
FOR WHAT THEY HAVE DONE

ARE YOU READY TO ACCEPT?
YOUR OWN FATE WHEN DEAD
WITHOUT DEMANDING A PERSONAL REQUEST

M.?. X - IV

ARE YOU DENYING ALL PLAUSIBILITY?
DEPENDING ON WHAT YOU CAUSED
BECAUSE OF YOUR ENDLESS DRAMA

THE BOOK IS OPENED
REVEALING ALL THE TRUTH
WHAT YOU HAD INSTITUTED

THE DEAD WILL BE JUDGED
FOR WHAT THEY HAVE DONE

ARE YOU READY TO ACCEPT?
YOUR OWN FATE WHEN DEAD

MR. X – IV

MR. X's Intimate Thoughts:

THE DECEASED ARE JUDGED
WITHOUT ANY LOST LOVE
CONSUMED WTHIN THEIR DETAILS

THE BLACK DESOLATE SEA
WILL CONTINUE TO OVERSEE
WHO PASSES THROUGH ITS GATES

THE DEAD WILL BE JUDGED
FOR WHAT THEY HAVE ENCOMPASSED

EVERY SOUL MUST CONFESS
WITHOUT DOUBT OR CONCERN
WHETHER RIGHT OR WRONG

THE OCEAN OF FIRE
BURNS AND DROWNS LIARS
WHO ENTER ITS WATER

THE DEAD WILL BE JUDGED
FOR WHAT THEY HAVE ENCOMPASSED

MR. X - IV

MR. X's Intimate Thoughts:

THE WALKING DEAD
AWAIT THEIR FINAL ENDING
IN CAGES OF FIRE

THE DEAD WILL BE JUDGED
FOR WHAT THEY HAVE OBSTRUCTED

DEATH AND HADES
FEED THE FIERCE FLAMES
WITH SOULS DUE DAMNATION

THE DEAD WILL BE JUDGED
FOR WHAT THEY HAVE OBSTRUCTED

MANKIND WILL CONCEDE
TO SUFFERING FOR ETERNITY
BECAUSE OF THEIR BETRAYALS

THE DEAD WILL BE JUDGED
FOR WHAT THEY HAVE OBSTRUCTED

MR. X - IV

I requested Sindee to give the facts if she knew of them about the CRAZIED mob's main man. Sindee stared at me afraid and nervously asked me why I yearned to know.

I stated that it would be fitting, to start-off with him as a first choice to begin my supremacy of amassing a body count of the evildoers and their co-conspirators throughout the entire wastelands of Russia. I especially made a point that the CRAZIED mob's main man would be my debut because of the despicable act performed on fifty of my Spetsgruppa comrades. Lastly, it would be a precursor to what transpired as MR. X an assassin to be feared and talked about as the 'Boogie Man' in every language throughout the wastelands of the world by the CHAINED, CONVERTED and CRAZIED. I would also become the centre of a mythos within all the ranks of the ONE GOVERNMENT regime.

Sindee pressingly stated to me that no living thing had been in the presence of the CRAZIED mob's leader named Manic long enough to talk about it, without first being disembowelled and eaten alive. Manic is a sociopath and an aborted YES Cyborg Collector Clone experiment of Chief Biomedical Engineer, Ivan Gott that turned out to be severely defective. She said it was casted around behind closed doors through the grapevine throughout the YES Cyborg Clone, YES Cyborg Breeder Clone and YES Cyborg Collector Clone communities, that Ivan Gott was infuriated with the failed YES Cyborg Collector Clone experiment. He without delay had it transported and locked away in solitary confinement indefinitely at Vladimir Central Prison (known as Vladimirsky Central) for dangerous criminals, which is about 100 miles northeast of Moscow.

I looked at her and snickered with a sly remark, that I was thoroughly going to relish in inflicting relentless pain and suffering to Ivan Gott when his time came to die! After I had spoken my 'two cents worth' about the individual, I instantly apologized to Sindee for interrupting her and kindly asked her to continue with the facts about CRAZIED mob's leader named Manic.

M?. X - IV

Sindee continued the consultation from the precise 'point in time' where I previously disrupted her by accident. A YES Cyborg Collector Clone's physical appearance features are, as follows; average 2.01 metres in height, 102 kilograms in weight, physically fit, black colour skin, and ivory white eyes with braided pearl white short hair, wearing a red and white checked pattern doctor uniform with shiny black combat boots. It is designed with phenomenal strength and 'lightning-quick' reflexes to subdue its host. Also, it is programmed with superior intelligence focused in the mastery of limitless surgical theories and procedures, to include precision ambidexterity abilities and languages adaptation.

The YES Cyborg Collector Clone always accompanies a YES Cyborg Breeder Clone when a 'Termination Order Protocol' (TOP) is to be carried out against a human being designated for elimination. When a YES Cyborg Breeder Clone completes the TOP and detaches itself from the selected human subject, the YES Cyborg Collector Clone would simultaneously remove that human host's brain and eyeballs while they were clinically still alive, immersing the items in a portable airtight 'Cryonic Suspension Briefcase' (CSB) filled with heparin (an anticoagulant) solution and transport it to Chief Biomedical Engineer, Ivan Gott's private laboratory.

As soon as the items arrive at Ivan Gott's private laboratory, they are removed and prepped through a cryopreservation process, in anticipation for when a YES Cyborg Breeder Clone is to give birth in a 'Delivery Emersion Acceleration Pool' (DEAM) to a single 'Semi-Human Clone', after 8 hours of conception. The original brain and eyeballs that were extracted from the deceased human host are without hesitation surgically implanted into a 'Semi-Human Clone'.

But, for some reason, Manic who is considered to be the first and original YES Cyborg Collector Clone project of Chief Biomedical Engineer, Ivan Gott turned out to be a notable mortifying misrepresentation of him as a ground-breaking revolution-

MR. X - IV

ist in advanced technology in both the engineering and medical field. Ivan Gott is the only one who has absolute knowledge of why Manic is faulty.

Sindee concluded the whole story with her account of the facts about Manic and also informed me that he has a 'right-hand man' named Schizo. Schizo is a former prison officer that used to work at Vladimirsky Central at the time Manic was locked away in solitary confinement indefinitely at the prison. Manic befriended Schizo during his stay there and with a droplet of his blood infected Schizo unknowingly, which metamorphosed him into the first CRAZIED. When Supreme, DEVIFETAN's ONE GOVERNMENT militia successfully invaded on 01 January 2029, at 12:00 hours throughout the entire planet earth called the "Invasion At High Noon", Schizo assisted Manic to escape from Vladimirsky Central.

I looked at Sindee as she fidgeted and looked back at me with her impeccable large shiny black eyes and thanked her for all the information provided pertaining to Manic. She replied that she was more than happy to contribute any way she could with reference to intelligence on Manic the CRAZIED mob's leader. She then inquired from me what my strategy was for her and me with getting rid of Manic altogether.

I explained to her that I was going to be outside in the vacant lot across the road from her upstairs flat, as soon as it became dark, so I could disguise myself as bait when the CRAZIED mobs came out to hunt for fresh human meat. Sindee inquired what her part was to be in relation to my plan in the evening. I stated to her that I needed her to stay put in her one bedroom upstairs flat because I did not want any harm to befall my dear friend and girlfriend. She laid her eyes on me filled with gratitude for what I said with relation to her.

When daylight started to fade away in the Khimki skyline around 17:30ish hours and the dark of night emerged I left Sindee's flat. Once outside, I crossed the road, walked to the central area

M.?. X - IV

of the vacant lot, sat down on its cold hard dirt ground and waited for the CRAZIED mobs to come upon my position. About an hour and a half had passed by, 19:00ish hours, when I heard the sounds of multiple roaring engines echo throughout the outskirts of the city from where I sat silent. Moments later, behind me off in the distance I overheard 'ear piercing' screams of terror, chainsaws open full throttle and barbaric laughs mocking those being inflicted with unrelenting pain.

As I sat static in the middle of the vacant lot listening to nonstop inexcusable brutality going on nearby, one pristine platinum grey colour Dartz Nagel Dakkar Luxury Off Road SUV, and two blood spattered, dented and filthy ebony colour Combat T-98 Armoured Luxury SUVs passed by me on the road on my left side. The lead Combat T-98 Armoured Luxury SUV's rear brake lights illuminated on the vehicle when it came to an abrupt stop and the other two vehicles behind it did the same. All three SUV vehicles executed speedy U-turns and headed back toward my location.

The three SUVs were approximately 100 metres from where I was posted when they turned their vehicle mounted NOPTIC Thermal Imaging Camera with Spotlight Forward-Looking Infrared (FLIR) imaging systems on me. The three SUVs raced toward me and came to a skidding stop around 15 metres from the spot that I remained seated on the cold hard dirt ground of the vacant lot. A total of three CRAZIED individuals exited the three SUV vehicles, rushed toward me brandishing Gerber Gator machetes, 65 centimetres in overall length that included the 43 centimetre black oxide coated high carbon steel blade with a saw-back and stainless frame with a tactile rubber grip, while deliberately squawking noisily like chickens at me. I observed a fourth CRAZIED individual step out of the pristine platinum grey colour Dartz Nagel Dakkar Luxury Off Road SUV as the other three CRAZIED individuals were converging on me. He was about 2.01 metres in height, 102 kilograms in weight, physically fit,

MR. X - IV

black colour skin, and ivory white eyes with braided pearl white short hair, wearing a blue black in colour Khimki police officer uniform with shiny black high-top boots, not a red and white checked pattern doctor uniform with shiny black combat boots, as he calmly followed behind the three CRAZIED individuals.

When the three CRAZIED individuals were within 5 metres from being 'right on top' of me I spontaneously sprung to my feet from the seated position I presently was in on the cold hard dirt ground. My quills instantaneously extended to their full height from every follicle, as a defence shielding mechanism on command as I became utterly enraged, my coarse wire-like woodland green hair, medium in length, that covered my scalp glowed and generated a low pitched humming noise; my eyes' sclera that was crimson red, iris bright green burnt bright, and my pupils resembling those of a snake shifted to being fully dilated.

I lowered my head and raised my left and right trapezius shoulder muscles to shield my head and neck in entirety with the quills extended to full height from my upper torso as I charged with both arms outstretched resembling wings on an airplane at the three CRAZIED individuals, whom darted toward me wielding their Gerber Gator machetes. Within a minute I made contact with all three of them and tore through them shredding them into little pieces which completely covered me in blood, bone fragments and bits of flesh. The assumed to be, the first and original YES Cyborg Collector Clone named Manic, leader of the CRAZIED mobs that was wearing a blue-black in colour Khimki police officer uniform with shiny black high-top boots, that calmly followed behind the three CRAZIED individuals I had torn through punctually stopped and studied me in astonishment.

I sped toward Manic as he stood stationary, 'hell-bent' on overpowering and slaying him for what for he and his CRAZIED mob horde had brutally done to the other of my Spetsgruppa comrades, that survived the fall from a Mil Mi-26 Russian heavy transport helicopter but were badly injured when we

MR. X - IV

landed on to Arena Khimki's football field before being dismembered alive, and their body parts stockpiled into CRAZIED's Black Meat Wagons and driven away. I was almost about to collide with him when he jumped out of my way and I missed striking him 'head on'. As soon as I skidded to a sudden halt, quickly spun around 180 degrees to continue to engage Manic, I felt a stinging sensation to the left-side of my head and a warm wetness from the middle of my cheekbone and down the entire side of my neck. I raised my left arm, touched the area of concern with the palm of my hand to discover my left ear had been sliced off by Manic with the Surgical Scalpel, Amputation Knife, 28 centimetres in size that he gripped in his left hand.

Manic bellowed a fiendish laugh at me that he had cut off my ear. I snarled at him, raised both my arms and discharged ten individual quills from the top sections of my forearms. He was able to dodge seven out of the ten quills that were fired at him from 'point blank range'. Three quills hit him though; entered in and exited out the other end of those areas they made contact with. One quill blew through Manic's front region of the left thigh muscle, the second quill completely demolished the left knee, quadriceps femoris and gastrocnemius muscles and the third quill burst through the right external oblique muscle just underneath the bottom area of the chest of the pectoral muscle which knocked him flat on his back.

I walked up to Manic where he lay on the cold hard dirt ground spitting up blood from his mouth, transformed my left and right hand and arm to elbow into two large double edge razor-sharp blades, stood over his body as he stared up at me stunned and amputated both his arms at the shoulders. Then I bent down, looked into his ivory white eyes as he looked back at me wide-eyed in shock, declared to him that this is payback for my fellow Spetsgruppa comrades that he and his CRAZIED mob crew brutally butchered alive at Arena Khimki's football field and with a swift stroke of one of the transformed large double edge razor-sharp blades I beheaded him.

MR. X - IV

I stepped over Manic's lifeless body, reached down with my left hand and snatched up his decapitated head by its braided pearl white short hair, picked it up out of a pool of blood on the cold hard dirt ground and strolled off with it. As I walked in front of Manic's pristine platinum grey colour Dartz Nagel Dakkar Luxury Off Road SUV with his driver seated in it, tongue-tied with dismay inside the vehicle behind the steering wheel of the driver compartment, I tossed Manic's head on to the front windshield and departed the vacant lot.

Mr. X's Intimate Thoughts:

I USED TO LIVE MY LIFE
IN THE SHADOWS OF DARKNESS
WITHIN A WORLD OF THE BIASED
WITHIN A WORLD OF THE HEARTLESS

BLOODSHED TELLS MY TALE

I WAS ENTANGLED IN THE MIDDLE
BETWEEN EVERYTHING RIGHT AND WRONG
WITHIN A WORLD OF THE UNCIVILIZED
WITHIN A WORLD OF THE LOST

BLOODSHED TELLS MY TALE

I FORESAW MY WAY TO PERFECTION
BY CLEANSING MYSELF OF IMPURITIES
WITHIN A WORLD OF THE SEGREGATED
WITHIN A WORLD OF THE FOOLISH

BLOODSHED TELLS MY TALE

Chapter V

Mr. X - V

First Aid Rendered, Modification Implemented and Plan Decided

After, I had chucked Manic's head on to the front windshield of his pristine platinum grey colour Dartz Nagel Dakkar Luxury Off Road SUV and departed the vacant lot, I speedily dashed 'out-of-sight' before the trauma diminished with the remaining CRAZIED mobs, whom witnessed what I had done to their leader.

Manic's 'right-hand-man' named Schizo arrived at the scene about fifteen minutes later where Manic's lifeless body lay in an extensive pool of blood on the cold hard dirt ground of the vacant lot. He collected up Manic's remains, put them in the trunk of his pristine platinum witching hour colour Dartz Nagel Dakkar Luxury Off Road SUV and departed the area.

I used the shadows of the night as concealment to cautiously travel back to Sindee's one bedroom upstairs flat. When I showed up at Sindee's front door to her dwelling, I lightly knocked on the door, softly whispered her name and identified myself. She softly answered in return to me to wait for a moment while the three deadbolt locks were unbolted so the olive green colour Security Panelled Single Front Door could be opened to let me inside. A little less than a minute and a half had lapsed when Sindee unlocked the front door that led into her one bedroom upstairs flat. The door knob turned counter-clockwise from the inside, it was hastily opened, she immediately ushered me inside, and I closed and locked it behind me.

Sindee looked fixedly in alarm at what I looked like completely covered from 'head to toes' in blood, bone fragments and bits of flesh from the three CRAZIED individuals I had torn through which shredded them into little pieces all over me. Also, my left ear was removed because it had been sliced off by Manic and

MR. X - V

dried blood stained the middle of my cheekbone and the entire left side of my neck. She asked me with a tone of tenderness in her voice if there was anything she could do for me.

I told Sindee yes there were a couple of things I would be very grateful of and indebted to her if she could do for me. She stared into my snake eyes with her large shiny black eyes with delight to give me a helping hand in fulfilling and satisfying my requests. I asked her if she could have a hot shower ready for me to enter under to wash off all the dry blood, bone fragments, and bits of flesh that I had all over me to include performing first aid with sewing up the open wound on the left side area of my head where my ear had been permanently detached once I had finished with taking the hot steamy shower. She vibrantly grinned with an eagerness of enthusiasm to get started right away with the tasks appointed to her by me.

I removed all personal items and valuables from the pockets of my clothing and discarded all my clothing into a black tall kitchen bin trash bag. I stepped under the hot water that sprayed out of the shower head in the bi fold, hinge, pivot-sliding shower door enclosure that had been prepared for me by Sindee and washed off the entire dry blood, bone fragments, and bits of flesh that had been all over me. When I finished scrubbing away every trace of dry blood, bone fragments, and bits of flesh from my body and cleaned the open wound on the left side area of my head to the best of my ability, I called out to Sindee if she was ready for me with what I needed for her to do that was necessary.

Sindee replied in return that she was in position and waiting for me in the kitchen. I dried myself off with the fluorescent lime and purple coloured, extra-large, 100% cotton luxury bath towel, wrapped it tight around my waist, secured it with a knot on my left hip and exited the bathroom to link up with Sindee in the kitchen. As I arrived in the kitchen, Sindee was seated in one of the slender metal framed chairs with dingy off yellow upholstery and had arranged on top of the kitchen table

𝒎𝒓. 𝒳 - 𝒱

a TMC Model 200R: Nymph & Dry Fly Straight eye fish hook, 138 (T135) (Tkt 20), .414mm nylon spindle sewing thread, a large, two handle copper-bronze water bowl filled with boiling hot sea salt water, two orange, cleaning hydrophilic sponges, a roll of plain white, 2-ply absorbent paper towels, a roll of pink and white polka dot, duct tape, 48 mm x 9.14 m, a small, fruits/vegetables-scrub brush and three 1000ml, 40.0% Alcohol By Volume (ABV) bottles of Putinka Classic Russian Vodka to use as expedient improvised items to do first aid with relation to cleaning, stitching and closing the open wound on the left side area of my head where my ear had been sliced off by Manic with a Surgical Scalpel, Amputation Knife, before I cut-off both his arms at the shoulders and his head.

 I grabbed the other slender metal framed chair with dingy off yellow upholstery, lifted it up and away from the narrow kitchen table. I set the chair down sideways with its backrest facing the outer edge of the kitchen table next to Sindee and positioned myself to where I straddled the seat of it. I turned my head in her direction, I looked into her large shiny black eyes and asked if she had ever stitched closed an open wound of any sort. Sindee grimaced and shook her head left to right with nervous affirmation that she had never performed anything even remotely similar as what she was about to do to me.

 I assured Sindee that I would guide her through each stage of the 'step-by-step' procedure to effectively perform first aid to the open wound on the left side area of my head. I grabbed one of the three bottles of Putinka Classic Russian Vodka, unscrewed off the twist cap, lifted the neck of the bottle to my slightly open mouth, took three large swigs from the bottle of vodka and placed it back down on top of the kitchen table with the cap removed. I glanced at Sindee, and then commenced with talking her through 'fixing me up' with the expedient improvised items available to correctly start and finish general surgery to the open wound I had unexpectedly received, as follows;

Mr. X - V

- Immerse one of the orange, cleaning hydrophilic sponges in the large, two handle copper-bronze water bowl filled with boiling hot sea salt water, wring out the excess sea salt water, carefully wipe around the outside of the wound and thoroughly inside it on the left side area of my head. Also, submerge the front section and with the bristles on the small, fruits/vegetables scrub brush in the water bowl, meticulously scrub the inside of the exposed meat of my open wound.
- Open one of the two unopened bottles of Putinka Classic Russian Vodka on top of the kitchen table, saturate the whole left side area of my head and the open wound where my ear once was before it had been sliced off, with half of the contents within the vodka bottle. The remaining amount of alcohol left inside the bottle pour out into a redwood colour, ceramic cereal bowl to repeatedly dunk the TMC Model 200R: Nymph & Dry Fly Straight eye fish hook to sterilize it before inserting 138 (T135) (Tkt 20), .414mm nylon sewing thread through the eye of the fish hook and tying it off, to stitch closed the open wound on the left side area of my head.
- Sew shut tight the open wound with the fish hook, and sewing thread which included the area of facial meat that frequently was gently dabbed and wiped away of blood that formed from each finished stitch pattern with a moist sheet of plain white, 2-ply absorbent paper towel dipped in the boiling hot sea salt water.
- Place two folded sheets of 2-ply absorbent paper towel over the total length of the sealed area of the wound and secure it in place along all four edges with torn off strips of pink and white polka dot, duct tape, from the 48 mm x 9.14 m, duct tape roll.

As soon as Sindee had completed the final set of instructions pertaining to successfully performing first aid to the open wound on the left side area of my head, she leaned over toward where

Mr. X - V

I was seated in the chair with its backrest facing the outer edge of the kitchen table, in a straddled position, kissed the left side of my neck and then knelt down on both knees. Then Sindee commanded me to unstraddle the chair and sit on it properly with my back pressed flush against its backrest. I did as I was ordered to do as she placed her left hand on the inside centre part of my left thigh and her right hand on the inside centre part of my right thigh; spread both my legs to allow ample width to expose my 'man-tool'. She put her head between my legs, commenced to orally arouse me with bioengineered stimulant saliva from her mouth until my 'man-tool' was fully erect and continued to go down on me until after a long duration of time, I intensely discharged every droplet of my internal liquid that she gladly swallowed. When the 'Depletion Extraction Empty Process' (DEEP) was successfully perfected on me, she glanced up at me and grinned with delight to what she able to accomplish for the both of us sexually.

Once Sindee had concluded with the 'task at hand' that she felt to be necessary, she stood up from her kneeling position between my legs and I asked her if she had knowledge of where I could acquire a clean new set of clothes to wear. She informed me that five doors down on the left side in another vacant flat that used to be occupied by a YES Cyborg Breeder Clone on the same floor as her one bedroom upstairs flat were several Intra/Extra Activity (IEVA), Body Temperature Control System (BTCS) latex skin fitting suits. She affirmed that these latex skin fitting suits would be a perfect fit for me to wear especially when my quills would extend on command when I became enraged or felt threatened, to their full height of 18cm from every follicle throughout my body, except from the base of my neck to the top of my head, when activated as a defence shielding mechanism. I also asked Sindee if she had any insight to where I could procure a wire mesh open face hood similar to what a knight wore in medieval times that covered the ears and entire

MR. X - V

neck to protect against enemy's sharp blade of choice in an attack, because the base of my neck to the top of my head was the most vulnerable unprotected area on me, even after I trigger the defence shielding mechanism. She said in the same vacant flat that was five doors down on the left-side from her one bedroom upstairs flat a CRAZIED mob, Scout Soldier regularly used it to bring back YES Cyborg Breeder Clones, he had drugged to have sex with while he bound and gagged them, until about three months ago when one freed itself and killed him.

I thanked Sindee for her assistance that was very useful to me in being able to properly clothe myself from being presently naked. I stood up from the slender metal framed chair with dingy off yellow upholstery, walked to her one bedroom upstairs flat, olive green colour Security Panelled Single Front Door as Sindee followed close behind me, exited the flat with her, strolled down the dim lit hallway to the vacant flat five doors from where she lived, opened the front door and the both of us entered inside it. Sindee and I entered the vacant flat, closed the door behind us and found it to be in a 'state of shambles'. There was furniture flipped over, broken glass, cockroaches, flies, mice and trash everywhere in every room throughout the vacant flat.

After about thirty minutes of us extensively rumaging around in the master bedroom of the vacant flat that was regularly used by the CRAZIED mobs, Scout Soldier and YES Cyborg Breeder Clones, I uncovered two Intra/Extra Activity (IEVA), Body Temperature Control System (BTCS) latex skin fitting suits (one lime green in colour and the other lipstick red in colour) on the floor of the bedroom walk-in closet buried underneath broken cardboard boxes filled with trash. Sindee found a wire mesh open face hood behind a two drawer bedroom nightstand in exceptional condition.

She handed over to me the wire mesh open face hood that was in exceptional condition she unearthed that was hidden in 'plain sight'. I applauded her for her vigilance in search of the

MR. X - V

items I needed for my new set of clothes to replace the old ones, which were completely covered and ruined in blood, bone fragments and bits of flesh. We both exchanged cordial smiles with one another as I led the way to the vacant flat, front door; then we exited it, walked through the dim lit hallway in the direction to Sindee's one bedroom upstairs flat with the olive green colour Security Panelled Single Front Door; we entered inside it, and Sindee shut the front door behind us and dead bolted it.

She took the lime and red IEVA and BTCS latex skin fitting suits that I had clutched, 'balled-up' in each one of my hands. She informed me that she was going to thoroughly wash the two latex skin fitting suits in the stainless steel kitchen sink with hot water, FAIRY antibacterial lime/lemongrass dish washing liquid, DEZMIR.RU industrial disinfectant solution and a cap full of Clorox ultimate care premium liquid bleach to get rid of any cockroach eggs, fly larva and mice faeces before I slip into one of them to wear.

I announced to Sindee that I was very appreciative and at the same time, I would be cleaning my all terrain black combat boots, then proceed to inventory, layout and perform serviceability checks on Vityaz-SN, semi-automatic and fully automatic, submachine guns, MP-443 Grach, double-action, short-recoil semi-automatic pistols, ammo shoulder harnesses, and vests with complete basic combat issued load, walkie-talkie phones and ZOOM 20-180 x100, HDMI night vision binoculars for the future plan I have envisioned for us to undertake with a successful outcome.

Sindee and I accomplished with ease our tasks within roughly fifty minutes. I called out to her from the bedroom where I conducted the inventory, layout and serviceability checks of all the equipment we had taken from the CHAINED-Security Building Patrol Clansmen (C-SBP-C) and CHAINED-Security Roving Foot Patrol Clansmen (C-SRFP-C) after the both us had swiftly slain them. I also requested if she could bring with her into the bedroom the one unopened bottle of Putinka Classic Russian Vodka. She returned with a reply of okay to my request before she headed toward and entered the bedroom.

When she walked into the bedroom, I pointed with my left fore and middle fingers to 'take a seat' in the old burgundy colour cloth upholstered armless bedroom chair that I set on the floor, one metre from the foot of the bed. Once Sindee was comfortably seated in the bedroom chair, I then revealed my future plan that I meant to carry out in a prompt and timely matter with true precision. I also indicated to her I very much desired for her to assist me, being considered a trustworthy partner to be counted on to achieve an unquestionable victory. Before I was able to unveil my actual future plan, she politely interrupted me to assure me that she was with me until 'death do we part' in whatever I maintained necessary to be done.

MR. X - V

MR. X's Intimate Thoughts:

SMILES ARE TURNED UPSIDE
AND CHANGED INTO FROWNS
TO PREVENT ANYONE RENOUNCING
THE REIGN OF THE WICKED
THE SCHEME IS JUST SICKENING

SIGNS OF WICKEDNESS
THEY LIVE FOR THIS
SIGNS OF WICKEDNESS
EVERY DAY IN EVERY WAY

DISSENSION HAS ERASED HARMONY
TO CREATE A MONOPOLY
SUITED FOR AN AUTONOMY
FOR REIGN OF THE WICKED
THE SCHEME IS JUST SICKENING

SIGNS OF WICKEDNESS
THEY LIVE FOR THIS
SIGNS OF WICKEDNESS
EVERY DAY IN EVERY WAY

MR. X - V

DISHONESTY NEEDS NO INTRODUCTION
LIES ARE ITS SIGNATURE
FALSIFYING THE FORTHRIGHT MISSION
A REIGN OF THE WICKED
THE SCHEME IS JUST SICKENING

SIGNS OF WICKEDNESS
THEY LIVE FOR THIS
SIGNS OF WICKEDNESS
EVERY DAY IN EVERY WAY

MR. X - V

MR. X's Intimate Thoughts:

HIGH UP IN THE SKY
INVISIBLE TO THE HUMAN EYE
HE LOOKS DOWN ON THE WORLD
WATCHING UNFAZED MANKIND BEING PURGED
LIFE AFTER LIFE WITHOUT REMORSE

A.O.D.
ANGEL OF DEATH

HIGH UP IN THE SKY
UNSEEN BOTH DAY AND NIGHT
HE SPREADS WIDE OPEN HIS WINGS
WITH APPARENT READINESS TO INHERENT
COLLECTING UP ON ANOTHER DEATH

A.O.D.
ANGEL OF DEATH

HIGH UP IN THE SKY
INVISIBLE TO THE HUMAN EYE
HE WITNESSES THE CONTINUOUS VICIOUS CYCLE
BOUNDLESS IN ENGINEERING FLAWLESS GENOCIDE
ATTEMPTING TO RULE OVER ALL

A.O.D.
ANGEL OF DEATH

DEATH IS HIS CALLING CARD

Chapter VI

MR. X - VI

Hit List Finalized and Plan Exercised

After Sindee had politely interrupted me before I disclosed my future plan to her that I was 'dead set' to carry out, she then urgently appealed to me to hear what I had to say with regards to it. She sat up straight in the old burgundy colour cloth upholstered armless bedroom chair that I set on the floor, one metre from the foot of the bed and keenly listened to everything I divulged to her. I also reiterated to her how I very much desired for her to aid me in accomplishing absolute victory being a credible partner that I knew I could wholeheartedly trust and count on without a 'second thought'.

The future plan to be exercised to absolute superiority was, as follows:

1. *Distribute, Fit and Arm* Sindee with the available resources present such as, an ammo vest with complete basic combat issued load, two shoulder harnesses (criss-cross each other when worn), four MP-443 Grach, double-action, short-recoil semi-automatic pistols, one Vityaz-SN, semi-automatic and fully automatic, submachine gun, one walkie-talkie phone and Russian Infantryman, digital flora dark in colour, Compact Tactical Backpack (CTB) with essential items stored in it. Sindee's transformation would not only be a change with relation to her physical appearance but also her name too that was given to her when activated to life as a YES Cyborg Clone by her maker, Victor Young. She will be reborn again effective immediately as MERC. Distribute me with current resources accessible such as, a walkie-talkie phone and one ZOOM 20-180x100, HDMI night vision binoculars. I once was a human being that was transformed into a mutant, the day

Mr. X - VI

Chief Biomedical Engineer, Ivan Gott, a devout high ranking member of ONE GOVERNMENT injected me with a serum, called 'Exodus Equals Erased' (E^3), a 100 % 'concentrate-in-pure-form'; atom-sized synthetic living organisms. These synthetic living organisms invaded my bloodstream forced into the jugular veins in my neck with the purpose to literally vaporize me into nothingness, but instead reshaped my mental and physical makeup that turned me into 30% human and 70% synthetic evolving energy (SEE). I too am reborn and my name **Роман Усов** (Roman Usov) no longer exists because henceforth I am 'Mr. X'.

2. *Vacate, Roam and Mask.* Sindee now known as MERC and me as Mr. X will leave behind our past lives and everything related with them. We will travel north, south, east and west throughout the vast wasteland within the borders of the country previously well-known as the Federal Subject of Russia and outside the fortified walls encircled around its capital city of Moscow. The both of us will disguise ourselves for the ulterior motive to freely employ undetected as ghosts among the CHAINED, CONVERTED and CRAZIED populace assassinating their hierarchy of leadership at will and unchallenged.

3. *Recognize, Rebuild and Reality.* MERC and Mr. X through our actions will serve as a testament that the power the wicked possess, that has a stranglehold over all of humanity, throughout the world is not permanent. All evildoers will be exposed for who and exactly how responsible they are for the level of carnage that has been inflicted on mankind whether human, half human or nonhuman. This self-named dynasty built on the foundation of putrid is going to come tumbling hard to the ground. It's Figurehead and Pawns are going to be unaware of being hunted and unprepared for the sudden death that overtakes and devours them as a whole, delivered by the бука (Buka), 'Boogie Man'.

MR. X - VI

The Hit List Finalized in order of priority had been influenced by the emphasis of those individuals unaccountable repeated acts that were significant in the destruction of life, as follows:

1. ONE GOVERNMENT's Chief Biomedical Engineer, Ivan Gott and recognized as a distinguished official of the regime.

Crimes committed by him are *genocide/mass murder and unauthorized experimentation* on human beings with a personally developed serum, called 'Exodus Equals Erased' (E^3). That is a 100 % 'concentrate-in-pure-form', atom-sized synthetic living organisms that invade the bloodstream by injection into the jugular veins of a person's neck. Also, *sexual assault* performed on female 'Young Easy Sex' (YES) Cyborg Clones through aggressive coercion.

2. ONE GOVERNMENT's Head Artificial Intelligence (AI) Inventor Victor Young and recognized as an eminent official of the regime.

Crimes committed by him are *contract killings, illegal organ harvesting/body parts snatching, identity theft and unauthorized creation of 'Semi-Human Clones'* to unaware human beings. The combination of these heinous wrongdoings were performed by YES Cyborg Breeder Clones when the directive by Victor Young was given for 'Termination Order Protocol' (TOP) which was then without delay carried out by YES Cyborg Breeder Clones against the selected person designated for elimination. As soon as YES Cyborg Breeder Clones are successfully finished with 'Termination Order Protocol' (TOP) and detached from the chosen human subject, YES Cyborg Collector Clones then execute its responsibility to simultaneously remove that human host's brain and eyeballs while they are clinically still alive, immersing the items in a portable airtight 'Cryonic Suspension Briefcase' (CSB) filled with heparin (an anticoagulant) solution and transport it to one of Chief Biomedical Engineer, Ivan Gott's local private laboratories.

Once the items arrive at one of Ivan Gott's private laboratories, they are then taken away to be prepped through a cryopreservation process, in anticipation for when YES Cyborg Breeder Clones are to give birth in a 'Delivery Emersion Acceleration Pool' (DEAM) to single 'Semi-Human Clones', after 8 hours of conception. The original brain and eyeballs that were extracted from the human host deceased and disposed of are without hesitation surgically implanted into 'Semi-Human Clones', that effective immediately is a permanent replacement of the perished individual. The TOP is a horrid monstrous step-by-step sequence function operated by YES Cyborg Breeder Clones upon male victims. Its prey's 'meat-pole' is forced to an erected state orally. Then as the prey remains erect, YES Cyborg Breeder Clones jump on top of it, force it inside them and begin the 'Vaginal-Vacuum Immobilization Participant Extraction Resources' (V-VIPER) that draws out every ounce of bodily fluid and semen. The sufferer is paralyzed in severe agony and sheer terror, as every ounce of bodily fluid and semen is forcibly extracted from the body. Additional to the offenses named is also, *sexual assault* performed on female 'Young Easy Sex' (YES) Cyborg Clones through aggressive coercion.

3. CRAZIED mob's leader, Manic's 'right-hand man' (second-in-command) named Schizo and praised with high esteem being the first living example of a human to be reborn as a CRAZIED from droplets of Manic's blood.

Crimes committed by him are *homicide* by butchering innocent people of all ages for sport to dissect and gorge on as a delicacy.

4. Vivian Young the twin sibling of Victor Young and devout representative of ONE GOVERNMENT.

Mr. X - VI

Crimes committed by her are *collaborator and co-conspirator* associated with Victor Young's wrongdoings, to include *exploitation, fraud and racketeering and sexual assault* performed on male 'Young Easy Sex' (YES) Cyborg Clones through aggressive coercion.

5. ONE GOVERNMENT Supreme, DEVIFETAN.

Crimes committed by him are *eradication and extermination* of the entire world's governments and everyone and everything related to them through brute force to establish a self-proclaimed dictatorship rule unopposed by anyone.

When I finished with the presentation in its entirety, MERC suggested that one more name be added to the finalized Hit List, as No. 1 instead of ONE GOVERNMENT's Chief Biomedical Engineer, Ivan Gott and to move him along with all the others down one, not to disrupt the order but to add to it. I projected a sly smile of agreement to her that I unanimously endorsed her proposal and eagerly asked who is it that we are to add to the Hit List as No. 1?

MERC stated that the individual's name is Pious, who appointed himself as the sole eminence of the CONVERTED group and founding father of House-Of-One cult. He is a fanatic that invokes a radical ideology, enacting human sacrifice and sadomasochism as the norm for those identified impure. For the first time since being introduced to Sindee now known as MERC, I witnessed a 'dark side' in her demeanour in that very moment. I placed both my hands on the top of her shoulders, softly massaged them, looked into her large shiny black eyes and asked with a tone of concern in my voice if she was okay.

MERC gazed in return into my crimson red sclera, bright green iris, pupils resembling those of snake eyes with a serious look on her face and explained why Pious must be added to the Finalized Hit List. She reminded me about Victor Young, who had ordered an 'Indefinite Deactivate Order' (IDO) on her ef-

ᎮR. X – VI

fective immediately because of her attempt to aid her client in evading a TOP designated for him, a well-known wealthy Media Mogul from Prague in the Czech Republic, who was visiting the city of Hong Kong for a round of business meetings. Also afterwards, when she awoke from the backhand given to her by a male YES Cyborg Collector Clone that lifted her up off her feet which caused her to hit her head off a metal frame of a large wall mounted mirror which knocked her out cold, she discovered that her pinkie fingers and toes on her left and right hand and foot were removed, which signified to everyone in the escort business and sex industry that she was indefinitely deactivated to provide any type of services, so she ended up wandering the slums of Hong Kong begging for food, money and shelter until one evening she met a young woman named Whisper. Whisper was a 21-year-old, 1.91 metre tall attractive Russian woman who weighed 54.9 kilograms, with 95J size breast implants, pale skin, fit body, green eyes and long straight red hair, who was a part-time exotic dancer and full-time professional musician that played bass guitar in an all-female Gothic Band called ОЗУ его вниз (Ram It Down), who befriended MERC. The band was recently finishing a mini tour that began in the city of Moscow, Russia on to the capital cities of Ulan Bator, Mongolia; Beijing, China; Vientiane, Laos; Bangkok, Thailand; Phnom Penh, Cambodia; Hanoi, Vietnam and was returning to the city of Moscow to 'wrap-up' the band's final show, when Whisper urged that MERC 'tag-along' with her to never have to live on the streets again.

MERC confessed that Whisper was a lifesaver to her because she helped her flee the miserable slums in the city of Hong Kong and the country of China to live a renewed pleasant life with her in the city of Khimki, Russia before the 01 January 2029, at 12:00 hours, "Invasion At High Noon" simultaneous genocidal chaos triumphantly executed by ONE GOVERNMENT relentless militia throughout the entire planet earth. She recited

MR. X - VI

that very soon after ONE GOVERNMENT rule became absolute in each country's capital and the rest of every country's remaining land territory was turned into nothing but a wasteland of ruins, is when Shackle's CHAINED sect, Pious' CONVERTED group and Manic's CRAZIED mob laid claim to their dominance all through the wastelands among the survivors, who were deprived the right as the élite, wealthy and those selected to be in servitude to these so-called proper people to live and work inside the fortified walls encircled around the capitals.

It was about nine months ago, when Pious and his CONVERTED group arrived in the city of Khimki in search of new recruits to be forcibly CONVERTED or deemed for a human sacrifice if identified as impure by his authority. Whisper was seen by a team of the CONVERTED exiting one of the CHAINED owned Gentleman Club establishments named 'WET & WICKED', they chased after, caught up with and took her away against her will to never come home ever again. MERC said with mixed anger and sadness in her voice that she was notified from a CHAINED-Security Enforcements Clansman (C-SE-C) that Whisper was sacrificed by Pious 24 hours after she was brought before him. MERC reiterated to me that is why she recommended that one more name be added to the Finalized Hit List and that she alone would bury a bullet between the eyes of Pious, the self-appointed sole eminence of the CONVERTED group and founding father of House-Of-One cult for wrongfully taking the life of her closest dear friend and thought of as a sister, Whisper.

I made it clear to MERC that I supported her position and there was 'no way in hell' an issue in relation to Pious being added to the Finalized Hit List. I also indicated to her that I looked forward to the moment and would be honoured to witness her deliver justice overdue to someone such as Pious.

MERC and I stood stationary in front of one other and gazed silently into each other's eyes for a brief minute before suiting up, collecting necessary items and arming ourselves with, that which

MR. X – VI

we were taking with us as we headed toward the olive green colour Security Panelled Single Front Door to permanently leave her one bedroom upstairs flat. After we entered into the dim lit hallway that led outside of her upstairs flat, I gave her one of the two black tall kitchen bin trash bags that were full that I was carrying, to help me take outside the building to discard of into the large dented up, rust covered metal grey dumpster located at the far end of the building complex parking lot. When the both of us exited the building, we walked up to the dumpster, tossed the two trash bags stuffed with; dry blood, bone fragments and bits of flesh-stained clothes of mine, luxury bath towel that I dried myself off with, expedient improvised items used to perform first aid on me, empty pale lager beer and classic Russian vodka bottles that were drunk out of and dirty plates with utensils that food was eaten off of. As I lit the trash bags on fire inside the dumpster to incinerate all traceable evidence that could or would be connected back to MERC and I, she turned to face the building and confessed to me with a saddened heart that for the first time since being activated to life, the one bedroom upstairs flat that her and Whisper lived in together was sincerely thought of as home even after the whole world was 'laid to waste' by ONE GOVERNMENT.

MR. X - VI

MR. X's Intimate Thoughts:

THE TIME HAS COME
FOR US TO LEAVE
BUT YOU HAVE TO BELIEVE
ALL WILL NOT BE FORGOTTEN
YOUR HEART WILL ACHE
TO LEAVE IT BEHIND
BUT YOU HAVE TO BELIEVE
TIME IS IN YOUR FAVOUR

DON'T WANT TO SAY GOODBYE
BUT YOU MUST

THE WINDS OF CHANGE
ARE CALLING OUR NAMES
BUT YOU HAVE TO BELIEVE
ALL WILL NOT BE FORGOTTEN
YOUR HEART WILL ACHE
TO JUST WALK AWAY
BUT YOU HAVE TO BELIEVE
YOU WILL RETURN ONE DAY

DON'T WANT TO SAY GOODBYE
BUT YOU MUST

Chapter VII

MR. X - VII

Hunting Commences and MERC Doesn't Hesitate

MERC and I departed the building complex parking lot 'on foot', after the two black tall kitchen bin trash bags, stuffed with items that could possibly be traceable back to us were engulfed within a fiery blaze inside the dumpster. We were prepared for our journey to the city of Pushkino, which is located 39.6 kilometres in the east from the city of Khimki, where we currently were at. The city of Pushkino northeast, (30 km) away from the capital of Moscow, used to be at one time, the Administrative Centre of Pushkinsky District in Moscow Oblast, Russia, positioned at a junction where the Ucha and Serebryanka Rivers equally converged with one another. The city nowadays is estimated to be 100% occupied, by hard-core members of the CONVERTED group true to House-Of-One cult radical ideology. Pious self-appointed sole eminence of the CONVERTED group took up residence at the Muranovo estate which was the Fyodor Tyutchev state museum in Pushkino, along with the many contents of historical important artefacts such as original artwork, furniture and manuscripts, which are all originals that belonged to Tyutchev, Baratynsky and their respective families. Pious' Headquarters for House-Of-One cult, the H-O² Seminary that prepares the unique chosen ones to invoke and provoke induced radical ideology as the basis for an exact beginning for a way of life and the Purity Temple Of Worship (PTOW) were all inside the 1678 year old erected, five-domed church of St. Sergius that was constructed at the manor of Komyagino.

By way of automobile travel at an average speed 50 km/per hour it would have taken 47 minutes to arrive at the destination, the city of Pushkino from Khimki. MERC and I did not have

ᛗ.?. X - VII

any form of transportation, so it took us 7 hours and 45 minutes to get there on foot. We trekked along in the cover of darkness to cloak ourselves from the CRAZIED mob's nonstop patrols while on the shoulder of roads E105/M10 to M8 through the city limits of Mytishchi, Korolyov and Tarasovka until we reached the outskirts of the city of Pushkino, where Pious and his CONVERTED group were based.

Once we reached our journey's end, positioned about 4.8 kilometres outside the city of Pushkino, I asked MERC if she had ever visited inside the city before. She slowly turned toward me and nervously said she had never left the city of Khimki, Russia since arriving with Whisper from the city of Hong Kong. I exhaled a breath of uncertainty with regards to entering the city blindly without any knowledge to the whereabouts of Pious at either the Muranovo estate or Kimyagino manor locations. MERC lowered her head with embarrassment for being impulsive without carefully thinking through the specific 'ins and outs' as to how she would 'track down' and confront Pious, 'face to face' before slaying him once we reached the city of Pushkino.

I playfully nudged the side of MERC's right shoulder with the side of my left shoulder and expressed to her not to be so hard on herself. I then explained to MERC that the both of us together as a duo would conduct an extensive in-depth reconnaissance, 360 degrees on the city of Pushkino. I also informed her that it would take about five exhausting full nights, working from sunset right through just before sunrise, but in the end Pious would be dead. She accepted the task that we would begin at nightfall.

As soon as the sun went down MERC and I embarked on day one of five with in-depth reconnaissance manoeuvres. At the conclusion of the fifth and final day of consecutively carried out tactical in-depth reconnaissance operations, we settled into our suitable camouflaged Observation Point (OP) to review all data collected for the final Reconnaissance Report (RECON-RPT).

ᎷᏃ. X – VII

The Reconnaissance Report (RECON-RPT) was, as follows:

LINE 1 – Reconnaissance Operations were conducted over a continuous five day mid-week, Wednesday through weekend, Sunday period. These reconnaissance missions began at sunset around 21:30 hours and ended around 03:30 hours, during the time of darkness.

LINE 2 – CONVERTED group Security Soldier-At-Arms (CGS-SAA) are designated as a 24/7 Presence Force that occupies checkpoints on all roads that lead into the city limits of Pushkino. CGS-SAAs are identified by the uniform worn; red skull cap, blue long-sleeved shirt and trousers and yellow high top boots. A senior CONVERTED group Security Soldier-At-Arms (CGS-SAA) officer, who is assigned to and in charge of each CGS-SAA squad. This individual recognized as being in a leadership position by the uniform worn; black skull cap, red long-sleeved shirt, blue trousers and yellow high top boots with black toe caps.

LINE 3 – Each CONVERTED group Security Soldier-At-Arms (CGS-SAA) squad are composed of 9 total personnel which includes the senior CONVERTED group Security Soldier-At-Arms (CGS-SAA) officer.

LINE 4 – The city of Pushkino is a closed administrative centre of Pushkinsky District in Moscow Oblast to all outsiders. Access granted inside it is by approval from a CONVERTED Security Force District Commandant only. Pushkino's residents are restricted from free movement to leave and return at will, without the accompaniment of a CONVERTED House-Of-One Appointed Chaperone. CONVERTED group Security Soldier-At-Arms (CGS-SAA) duties and responsibilities performed are enforcement to compliance of laws without exception pertaining to motorized or non-motorized travel in and out of the city, to include the use of lethal force when thought to be necessary. CGS-SAA shifts are twenty hours on and twenty hours off. A three man team (driver, gunner and truck commander) patrol the city perimeter (appointed checkpoint to next designated checkpoint to return to appointed checkpoint) every six hours in a GAZ-2330 Tigr 4x4 multi-role, all-terrain light armoured vehicle armed with a 7.62mm/12.7mm machine gun and 30mm automatic grenade launcher in reserve. The all-terrain light armoured vehicle while patrolling is always using its headlamps ('white lights') and never its tactical headlamps ('blackout drive') in infrared illuminator activation.

LINE 5 – There are a total of four Checkpoints (North, South, East and West) with Traffic Control Points (TCPs); N-A1, S-B2, E-C3 and W-D4, have been established on the main roads that lead into the city limits of Pushkino. All other paved and unpaved roads are considered minor routes that have been closed and barricaded with a massive 15 metres tall erected concrete guard tower in addition to being thoroughly mined (OZM-72, anti-personnel, affixed tripwires and TM-72, anti-tank mines) for a stretch of 500 metres starting at 25 metres out from the front of the guard towers.

LINE 6 – Pious the self-appointed sole eminence of the CONVERTED group has an active security force that is adequately armed as a measure for protecting and preserving the way of life of the CONVERTED group populace, its House-Of-One cult radical ideology within the isolated city of Pushkino. This security force is known as the CONVERTED group Security Soldier-At-Arms (CGS-SAA), comprised of serving members under the leadership of CONVERTED group Security Soldier-At-Arms (CGS-SAA) officers and command authority of a CONVERTED Security Force District Commandant.

Mr. X - VII

LINE 7 – The times of activity being performed by the CONVERTED group Security Soldier-At-Arms (CGS-SAA) that was observed was during a continuous five day mid-week, Wednesday through weekend, Sunday period from sunset around 21:30 hours and ended around 03:30 hours, span of darkness. This intelligence probing had to be temporarily discontinued each time from 03:31 hours through 21:29 hours because of daylight which could possibly jeopardize reconnaissance operations by 'giving away' its two members' surveillance team position.

LINE 8 – Each member of the CGS-SAA is equipped with two side arms, Fort 17 semi-automatic pistol, 9×18mm Makarov cartridge with four 13 round box magazines for each pistol (totalling 104 rounds) to include LT-6A accessory gun-mounted below the barrel flashlight. A NRS-2 exceptional survival knife with a built-in single-shot firing mechanism created to discharge a 7.62x42mm SP-3 (СП-3) bullet is also a standard issue given to every CGS-SAA individual.

Checkpoints (North, South, East and West) with Traffic Control Points (TCPs); N-A1, S-B2, E-C3 and W-D4 are manned with two RPK-74, 5.45×39mm calibre machine guns with four 45-round box magazines and additional eight 40-round curved magazines. Also two stationary Twin Head Tripod Halogen Flood Lights are positioned out in the direction of the road to illuminate for oncoming traffic.

The erected concrete guard towers put in place as a barricade to permanently eliminate passage on all minor routes of paved and unpaved roads into the city are manned with one Kord-12.7 mm heavy machine gun with SPP-M machine gun sight for shooting during daylight, twilight and night-time hours up to total distance of approximately 2000 metres utilizing graticule illumination, mounted on 6T7 folding ground tripod with six 50-round linked belts. Two RPG-32 multipurpose grenade

MR. X – VII

launchers, 105 mm calibre barrel and 72/105 mm warhead disposable ammunition with effective range 700 metres on a concealed or exposed target are accessible to CGS-SAA two man guard tower teams.

The CGS-SAA three man patrol teams that perform patrolling shifts on the city perimeter (appointed checkpoint to next designated checkpoint to return to appointed checkpoint) every six hours are equipped with three AK-12 assault rifles, 7.62×39mm included four 30-round detachable box magazines for each rifle issued, a GAZ-2330 Tigr 4x4 multi-role, all-terrain light armoured vehicle armed with contained standard package detachable turret mounted 7.62mm/12.7mm machine gun and 30mm automatic grenade launcher in reserve.

LINE 9 – *Credence* and *Quality* of *Information* gathered from the source of MR. X and MERC is positively accurate that is applicable to Pious and his CONVERTED group population that reside within the closed self-sufficient city of Pushkino, protected by the CGS-SAA appointed 24/7 Presence Force.

LINE 10 – The *Review* of the Reconnaissance Report (RECON-RPT) information by MR. X and MERC and discussed between the both of them clearly signify that covert access into the city of Pushkino to find Pious at either the Muranovo estate or Kimyagino manor locations to assassinate him was not impossible. But, exact knowledge of the city's interior layout is mandatory once infiltration is achieved by MR. X and MERC or capture and/or death could be highly probable.

LINE 11 – In *CONCLUSION*, there is a *Solution* to the matter in question with relation to obtaining overall insight to the city's interior layout, Pious' whereabouts at Muranovo estate or Kimyagino manor locations, his Headquarters for the House-Of-One cult, the H-O2 Seminary and the Purity Temple Of Worship (PTOW) all inside the five-domed church of St. Sergius at the manor of Komyagino, as immediate gain access is obtained.

This *Solution* can certainly be attained by carrying out a 'Snatch-And-Grab' (SAG) night mission to abduct, interrogate and terminate the life of a senior CGS-SAA officer.

LINE 12 – There is no additional essential information to report for clarification with regards to the Reconnaissance Report (RECON-RPT).

LINE 13 – It is confirmed that the Reconnaissance Report (RECON-RPT) has been permanently concluded and all its sensitive information will be indefinitely disposed of, effective immediately.

MR. X – VII

MR. X's Intimate Thoughts:

YOU MUST SURELY KNOW EVERY BROTHER
YOU MUST SURELY KNOW EVERY SISTER
WHAT YOU HAVE BECOME
WHAT IT HAS COST
FOR YOU AND INTO THE FUTURE

WHAT MADE YOU DECIDE
TO CAUSE YOUR OWN DEMISE
AND TURN YOUR LIVES
UPSIDE DOWN
INSIDE OUT
TO BECOME VICTIMS OF UNREST?

YOU MUST SURELY KNOW EVERY BROTHER
YOU MUST SURELY KNOW EVERY SISTER
WHAT YOU HAVE PERPLEXED
WHAT IS COMING NEXT
FOR YOU AND INTO THE FUTURE

WHAT MADE YOU DECIDE
TO IMPRISON YOUR OWN FREEDOMS
AND TURN YOUR LIVES
UPSIDE DOWN
INSIDE OUT
TO BECOME VICTIMS OF UNREST?

MR. X - VII

MERC concurred with the solution to do a SAG night mission to abduct, interrogate and terminate the life of a senior CGS-SAA officer. She then leaned in toward me where I knelt, playfully winked her large shiny black size eyes, moved in as to kiss me but gently bit down on my lower lip and firmly grabbed hold of my crotch area of the lime green colour Intra/Extra Activity (IEVA), Body Temperature Control System (BTCS) latex skin fitting suit with her left hand for a few seconds as she seductively smiled. Afterwards, she immediately gave me a passionate kiss on my lips, jumped to her feet, performed a full length stretch and stated she was ready for the undertaking as soon as it became nightfall.

When it turned to darkness outside, MERC and I left the OP to carry out an effective SAG night mission of a senior CGS-SAA officer. We arrived approximately 100 metres northeast from the North Checkpoint and N-A1 Traffic Control Point (TCP), and found an unsuspected, 'soft target' senior CGS-SAA officer that had leisurely strolled out-of-sight from his squad to urinate. MERC and I silently but speedily moved toward him to overcome him as he commenced to relieve himself. When the senior officer finished his business, I suddenly seized him from behind and performed an air choke that cut off air from his windpipe to his lungs which caused him to lose consciousness. He collapsed in my arms; I tossed him on to my shoulders and executed a fireman's carry with him draped across the top part of my back secured behind my neck and we cunningly dashed into the night away from the North Checkpoint and N-A1 Traffic Control Point (TCP) undetected by the CGS-SAA squad on shift at that site.

Once, back inside our decent camouflaged OP, MERC rapped a couple of times on the barrel of one of her MP-443 Grach, double-action, short-recoil semi-automatic pistol off the senior CGS-SAA officer's forehead until he awoke as he was bound and gagged. He lazily opened his eyes with a grimace to see MERC staring at him with a fierce expression on her face. The senior CGS-SAA officer then exhibited utter fear when he saw MERC and started

ᛗ.ℐ - VII

squirming to free himself from being restrained. MERC squatted over him, sat down with all her weight, deliberately slowly gyrated on his groin as she straddled him with the muzzle of the MP-443 Grach, double-action, short-recoil semi-automatic pistol pressed flush against the centre of his forehead and advised him to relax before she pulled the trigger.

The senior officer promptly laid still after MERC recommended he be at ease but continued to express utter fear as he looked up at her. MERC ordered him to answer a series of specific questions that she was going to ask him and suggested that it would in his best interest not hesitate or refuse to do so once the gag was removed from his mouth.

MERC initiated the set of questions with concern that focused on the complete blueprint layout inside the closed self-sufficient city of Pushkino, its notable landmarks, the renowned Pious' home at Muranovo estate, his Headquarters for House-Of-One cult, the H-O2 Seminary, the Purity Temple Of Worship (PTOW) all within the 1678 year old erected, five-domed church of St. Sergius that was constructed at the manor of Komyagino and total occupancy of CONVERTED group population that reside within the city. These set of questions included when, where and how does Pious travel throughout the large town every day. The senior CGS-SAA officer continuously recited his name, rank and CONVERTED group induction number after every question, MERC demanded an answer during the interrogation, which 'dragged on' like a 'broken record' over and over again for about ten minutes before I had heard enough of the individual's nonsense and mentioned to her that we did not have any more time to waste on the brainwashed idiot. At that very moment, MERC handed me the MP-443 Grach, double-action, short-recoil semi-automatic pistol, then firmly held the senior CGS-SAA officer's head in her hands, palms inward, with applied pressure to the left and right temples, and administered the 'Universal Line Equal Trade Multiple Effect' (U-LET-ME)

MR. X - VII

to procure by force all of his thoughts instantaneously. He went into a comatose trance as soon as she began to collect and receive all of his thoughts and once the U-LET-ME technique had finished she swiftly broke his neck, killing him in an instant.

MERC stood up from the seated straddle position on the senior CGS-SAA officer's groin, dismounted it, stepped away from his lifeless dead body that laid face up on the compacted clay floor of the concealed camouflaged OP, turned toward me, kindly asked me to give back the MP-443 Grach, double-action, short-recoil semi-automatic pistol of hers that I clutched in my left hand, while she had effectively performed the U-LET-ME technique on him. As I handed over the pistol to her, she told me that she knew where Pious would be tonight, approximately two hours from now and how we could meet up with him without being spotted by any CONVERTED group member, so she could terminate his existence with a bullet fired into his head from one of her four MP-443 Grach, double-action, short-recoil semi-automatic pistols. Pious would be at the Muranovo estate that he has assessed to be his home, routinely in his study, every evening around 21:30 hours until about 02:00 hours to review, revise and rewrite necessary Insight Amendments (IA) to the House-Of-One Demiurge-Constitution (D-C). She also assured me that she knew the full layout inside the closed self-sufficient city of Pushkino and where everything was situated once we snuck in stealth mode past the CONVERTED group Security Soldier-At-Arms (CGS-SAA) 24/7 Presence Force.

Before MERC and I conducted our individual pre-warfare serviceability checks and battle buddy inspections of each other's equipment, she conveyed to me that she was curious to find out if I had the ability to freely do something at will. I inquired with a puzzled look where she stood in front of me, of what she desired to know about a potential skill I might be able to execute.

She mentioned about the preliminary tests that were conducted by her on me, specifically the second test with relation to adjustment and regulation of my body temperature when she put the flame of a Zippo lighter to my fingertips and they did not burn or discolour, but alternatively the inside case of the lighter began to melt. She stated the test established that the pigmentation of my grey skin, onyx black fingernails, lips and tongue were sensors able to manipulate at will unlimited variances in fluctuation to distal-to-proximal temperature gradients and the unlimited number of these temperature variations are powered by the P300 (P3) waves evoked by the automatic stimulus process of vigilant decision making within my central nervous system. So, she wondered if I also possessed the capability to perform at will physiological colour change by the manipulation of the bands of my pigment cells causing an accelerated action of shifting and reshuffling of the cell membranes to create a physical change in colour as means of camouflage.

MERC outstretched her left arm, requested that I grab a hold of it, concentrate and attempt to perform a physiological colour change to turn my skin the same orange colour as hers. I gripped her wrist with my right hand, implemented the Calm, Collective, Control and Focus (C^3F) technique and right away changed the colour of my skin that was equal to MERC's. She immediately exhibited a big smile and commented that she had a notion I could perform at will physiological colour change aka Carbon-Copy-Camouflage.

I released the grip that I had on MERC's left wrist and the both of us started our individual pre-warfare serviceability checks. When we finished with the pre-warfare serviceability checks, we then moved on to the battle buddy inspections of each other's equipment and after that was concluded, we exited the camouflaged OP together and began to make our way to the South Checkpoint and S-B2 Traffic Control Point (TCP) which was closest in the vicinity of Pious' home at Muranovo estate. We were approximately 125 metres southeast from the paved road that led up to the entrance of South Checkpoint and S-B2 TCP. I

MR. X - VII

turned to MERC and softly whispered loud enough only for her to hear to jump on to my back, hold on tight to either my shoulders or around the base of my neck, for I was going to give her a 'piggy back' ride, as I performed a physiological colour change so we could pass by the CGS-SAA squad manning the South Checkpoint and S-B2 TCP undetected while in their presence. MERC acknowledged my recommendation, jumped on to my back, grasped firmly both of my shoulders as I provided her with a 'piggy back' ride, promptly performed a physiological colour change and briskly walked through the South Checkpoint and S-B2 TCP unnoticed.

Approximately 300 metres away from the South Checkpoint and S-B2 TCP that MERC and I had trekked through with ease unseen, MERC jumped off of my back, landed on both feet, then pointed to an elaborately constructed lit up building that was not too far off in the distance at our 1 o'clock direction and told me that it was the residence of Pious.

I recognized the fact, it was to be so and reminded her that the senior CGS-SAA officer that we did a SAG to, lying dead back at the OP had been missing from his assigned post, the North Checkpoint and N-A1 Traffic Control Point (TCP) for about one hour fifteen minutes. MERC admitted with absolute agreement that assassinating Pious must be done promptly before we lost the element of surprise and were discovered by the CONVERTED group Security Soldier-At-Arms (CGS-SAA) 24/7 Presence Force, which could result in us being captured or becoming trapped inside the closed self-sufficient city of Pushkino.

I securely grabbed MERC's left wrist with my right hand, performed a physiological colour change and together we rushed in unison toward the elaborately constructed lit up building, identified as the Muranovo estate, which was the home of Pious. MERC and I arrived in front of the Muranovo estate, across the street, on the concrete walkway within five minutes. I scanned the entire building (top to bottom/front to back and left to right) to include its grounds (front and back) using my thermal vision sensory to detect for all silhouette heat signatures that would be present inside and outside with my eyes resembling those of a snake. I described in a whisper tone of voice to MERC as I pointed with the forefinger on my left hand where every one of Pious' Personal Security Detail Personnel (PSD-P) were positioned throughout the Muranovo estate, as follows;

- Four PSD-P were outside on the rooftop, one at each corner of it.
- Four PSD-P were inside the main hallway that led to the interior of the building, two at the entrance/exit for control of access and egress, and two at the end of the corridor to oversee all 'foot traffic' for the full length of it.
- Two PSD-P were right outside a sizable room, on the ground floor, at the far end, centre inner area of the building. Its location is believed to be the study room of Pious. +NOTE+ Within the room was one giant silhouette heat signature and five little silhouette heat signatures.
- Three PSD-P were in the centre region of the basement, directly below the ground floor lobby, presumed to be PSD-P Command Operations Centre and lounge area.

MERC whispered in return her praise for the meticulous observation report of every PSD-P's immediate whereabouts revealed to her and informed me that the tactical approach we were going to carry out with sound precision was to enter inside the Muranovo estate, 'through the front door' per se, unchallenged, and unseen for her to triumphantly kill Pious.

MERC and I accomplished with effective superiority her intent in regards to the distinct tactical approach, until it was almost jeopardized when we entered the ground floor lobby. She came to a sudden halt without prior notice when she became disturbed by what she saw once we accessed the ground floor lobby. Along, all eight walls of the octagon shaped lobby were stuffed

MR. X - VII

'adult aged' naked people both male and female on display as if they were wild game animals hunted for sport with a gold aluminium placard screwed into the centre of their foreheads with information on it (name, location captured and House-Of-One judgement against their sins committed). MERC recognized that her closest dear friend Whisper, who had been taken away against her will, about nine months ago, never to come home ever again was one of these murdered people on display.

I almost lost the grip that I had on MERC's left wrist with my right hand, when she unexpectedly scampered to examine Whisper where she was set out as an exhibit in the ground floor lobby at the Muranovo estate of the residence of Pious. MERC muttered under her breath as she gazed at the murdered body of Whisper, that she would be avenged for the senseless wrongdoing done to her. MERC turned toward me with a bloodthirsty look of revenge and whispered that she was going to, without hesitation, blow Pious' fucking brains out. We exited the ground floor lobby, stealthily passed by the two PSD-Ps, invisible to them even though they were posted right outside the study room of Pious and entered the room unimpeded.

Once inside the room, MERC and I saw Pious, a hairless, bald headed, albino, with a shapely muscular physique, 2.7 metres tall and weighing 159 kilograms, with a chest to lower abdomen section covered in thick black tribal art tattoos. He, stood behind a well constructed large desk made out of redwood and coated in thick layers of lacquer. Five of his concubine women, who had half of their head shaved bald, with their faces painted as a smiling clown, naked except for yellow thigh high latex leather boots were also present in the room with Pious. His black leather full length hooded robe was unbuttoned and opened to expose his fully erect 13" 'man-tool' that two females while on their knees were repeatedly pleasuring orally. After a couple of minutes had elapsed, he then pulled his 'man-tool' away from the females that were knelt down on the floor and repositioned

MR. X - VII

it for the other three females bent over the large desk, face down with their chests pressed into it and legs spread shoulder width apart, exposing their smoothly shaved 'love-boxes' as he entered inside them with continuous hard thrusts.

MERC shook loose the grip of my right hand that was firmly attached to her left wrist, appeared in front of Pious on the front side of the well constructed large desk made out of redwood and coated in thick layers of lacquer, said the word "Boo". "This is for Whisper," she announced. Cool-headed, she pointed the MP-443 Grach, double-action, short-recoil semi-automatic pistol at Pious, squeezed the trigger, fired off a single round that hit him between the eyes and splattered debris of his brain matter out the back end of his skull on to the white wall behind him where he stood.

The five concubine women screamed out loud with panic as Pious dropped dead on to the three females that were bent over the large desk. I grabbed MERC's left wrist with my right hand again, performed a physiological colour change as we pivoted around together, sprinted passed the two Personal Security DETAIL PERSONELL (PSD-P), who rushed into the study room of Pious that were posted right outside, through the ground floor lobby, down the main hallway and outside the building of the Muranovo estate undetected by the Personal Security Detail Personnel (PSD-P) of Pious, whom all them raced to his aid.

Chapter VIII

MR. X - VIII

Who Is Next? It Could Be You ...

After, MERC and I exited the Muranovo estate altogether, invisible to the entire Personal Security Detail Personnel (PSD-P) that were attempting to calm the situation of commotion and sort the state of confusion pertaining to Pious being assassinated, we seen the broad-beamed, high-intensity outdoor floodlights illuminate throughout the whole closed self-sufficient city of Pushkino.

I tightened my grip on MERC's left wrist with my right hand, as I continued to perform physiological colour change, looked right at her and in a soft tone of voice instructed her that we were going to move 'with a purpose' to egress the city by the same route, South Checkpoint and S-B2 Traffic Control Point (TCP) as it was accessed prior. MERC without making a sound acknowledged me with a wink of approval. We expeditiously departed the city of Pushkino unopposed and continued to travel on foot, while in physiological colour change mode on the shoulder of the M8 road, until we reached the city limits of Tarasovka, 1 hour and 39 minutes later. I released the hold that I had on MERC's left wrist with my right hand while straight away deactivating the physiological colour change to the both of us since the first time it was initiated for its covert purpose.

MERC turned to me to convey that she was exhausted and hungry. I frankly admitted to her that I too was hungry. MERC and I noticed that the city of Tarasovka seemed entirely desolate of people as if everything in it closed at sundown, but we saw off in the horizon to the southeast a huge flashing neon sign for a nightclub called the GALACTICA.

We looked at one another and together reckoned that if there was not any type of lodging available 'to catch zees' for a couple

M.R. X – VIII

hours, at least food and drink would be accessible at the establishment. I asked MERC what type of currency we were going to use to pay the bill for what we had eaten and drunk. She affectionately smiled, placed her orange colour silky skin hands on the left and right cheeks of my face, laughingly squeezed them, kissed me on the tip of my nose and commented that she had it covered. Then MERC reached down into the front of the faded dark olive green Skinny Puppy industrial rock group, short sleeve t-shirt underneath the ammo vest she had on with her left hand. She pulled out from between her firm, medium in size, muscular orange colour breasts a red nylon little pouch with drawstring, which contained fifteen polished oval black onyx gemstones and referred to them as our source of money to buy ourselves a hot meal, and a cold beverage. I satisfyingly smiled in return and the both us headed southeast, in the direction of the huge flashing neon sign, where the nightclub called the GALACTICA was located.

It took MERC and me approximately 30 minutes to reach the front entrance of the nightclub while travelling on foot. At the front door, outside were two big burly, long haired and bearded, stout doormen, covered in tattoos that stood guard to scrutinize incoming patrons and serve as a deterrent measure to any troublemakers seeking to infiltrate the premises. Each one of the nightclub's doormen was armed with a AEK-919K Kashtan, 9mm, compact submachine gun, attached with a PMS silencer muzzle, loaded with one 30 round magazine inside its magazine well and stored in their black leather vests, left and right side pockets were an additional three more 30 round magazines.

When we approached the entrance into the nightclub called the GALACTICA, one of the big burly, long haired and bearded, stout doormen, covered in tattoos met us approximately 3 metres from the sparkling golden solid wooden front door that led into the club, and demanded MERC and I 'state-our-business' for desiring to enter the nightclub. MERC told him we sought to enjoy having a hot meal, and a cold beverage. The doorman

MR. X - VIII

glared at the both of us for about a minute, studying our appearance, then in an instant revealed a menacing smile, stepped aside to the left of us to allow us to pass by and stated to enjoy the food and drink that GALACTICA had to offer.

The second big burly, long haired and bearded, stout doorman, covered in tattoos that stood guard at the sparkling golden solid wooden front door of the nightclub, opened it for us and we walked inside the establishment to the sound of loud Pink Floyd music, and flashing neon strobe lights that filled the room. I leaned over to MERC's left-side, with a raised tone of voice loud enough to hear in her left ear, proposed to her to head to the bar, order our food and drink, and I would find us a table in the far right corner of the room, on the other side of the dance floor, accessible to the rear fire exit door. She nodded her head up and down in agreement, and made her way over to the designated area of the bar where customers in the nightclub could place their orders. I casually moseyed through the crowd of people as they rhythmically grooved on the dance floor to music, headed to an unoccupied table in the darkest far right corner section of the room closest to rear fire exit door. I had a clear line of view of the main entrance /exit of the GALACTICA nightclub, once I sat down with my back against the wall and waited for MERC to return, after she had placed our order with an available waitress at the bar.

MERC placed our order at the appointed food station of the bar with a waitress and made her way to the table I had chosen for us. She enlightened me that the food menu had only three items on it to pick from; Shashlik (marinated rabbit on skewers included with bell pepper, onion, mushroom and tomato), Rassolnik (soup made from pickled cucumbers, pearl barley and wild boar kidneys) and Solyanka (thick spicy sour soup containing mystery meat with pickled cucumbers, lemons and onions). She said she selected two orders of Shashlik and Rassolnik for the both of us to consume along with an unopened

MR. X - VIII

750 ml bottle of 100 Proof (black label), Ruskova vodka which cost three polished oval black onyx gemstones. I thanked her for the food and drink she had paid for in full with the three polished oval black onyx gemstones. Within 25 minutes another waitress who was assigned to work one half segment of the floor delivered our food and drink order to the table we occupied, and MERC expressed gratitude to her. After the waitress left, MERC sorted out the bowls and plates of food for us. I assisted her by opening the bottle of vodka and pouring it into two glasses half full for us.

As MERC and I were about to chow down on the bowl of Rassolnik, and plate of Shashlik, I asked MERC, filled with great interest, how she was able to absorb and use chewed up food that entered her body by way of the digestive tract, being a Yes Easy Sex (YES) Cyborg Clone. She explained to me that even though the internal and external design structure of her body is artificially enhanced to a degree beyond that of a human being, her biological framework is organic, which requires food as a fuel source to continuously function normally to remain alive. MERC also divulged that unlike a female, YES Cyborg Breeder Clone, who is designed with a reproductive system for the main purpose to breed and give birth to Semi-Human Clones, by enacting either Termination Order Protocol (TOP) for Human Replacement Integrations (HRI) or Transfusion Receiver Allocation Protocol (TRAP) for Blackmail and Distortion Collections (BDC), she was created without one. She went on to further explain with utter disdain that when a YES Cyborg Breeder Clone is impregnated by the scheme for TOP, it gives birth to a single Semi-Human Clone, within 8 hours of conception, that will be flawlessly identical to its human counterpart it will replace. If a YES Cyborg Breeder Clone is impregnated by the other scheme for Transfusion Receiver Allocation Protocol (TRAP), it again gives birth but to triplets of Semi-Human Clones, within 72 hours of conception, that too will be flawlessly identical to their human surrogate father that they will never get to know doing their existence.

Every Semi-Human Clone born from Transfusion Receiver Allocation Protocol (TRAP) are directly given to ONE GOVERNMENT and they are immediately enrolled into the Military Integration Learning Knowledge (MILK) Training Academy. They attend and graduate from a thirteen week MILK Training Academy course, then soon afterwards become registered ONE GOVERNMENT Soldiers.

I grabbed my half full glass of Ruskova vodka off the table, tilted it to my open mouth and guzzled half its contents and commented that what she had just explained to me was disturbingly genius in a figurative way. I set my half drunk glass of Ruskova vodka back down on to the table, emphasized to MERC that I did not mean to sound discourteous and distasteful, but was curious to know from her what happens to the leftover waste from food after digestion. MERC snickered and asked me if I was referring to human bodily waste, in the form of urine or caca. I replied yes to her question.

She clarified for me that every morsel of food she consumed was appropriately used within her body with a 0% waste result outcome. She reminded me that before being permanently deactivated, she once was an active Yes Easy Sex (YES) Cyborg Clone named Sindee, created and designed by her maker Victor Young for the sole purpose of monopolizing the global supply and demand in the escort business and sex industry. Her maker Victor Young awarded all female YES Cyborg Clones with a normal stimulus functioning vagina and anus for male client sexual gratification, but minus a urethra, bladder, sigmoid colon and large intestine.

I again grabbed the half empty glass of Ruskova vodka off the table, tilted it to my open mouth, guzzled the remainder of the contents and set it back down on to the table. I reopened the bottle of vodka, poured myself another glass, half full, of the

MR. X - VIII

100 Proof liquor and again commented that what she had described in detail to me was a representation of perverse intellect.

MERC and I devoured every bit of substance in the bowls of Rassolnik, and on the plates of Shashlik until there was nothing that remained. MERC got the attention of the waitress, who had delivered our food and drink order to the table to come over and collect up the dirty dishes, to take all of them away. When she arrived where we were seated at the table, MERC inquired what time the nightclub, GALACTICA was going to close. The waitress replied that the nightclub was open 24 hours a day except for Sunday, when the establishment was given a thorough cleaning, stockrooms resupplied and behind the bar replenished. MERC conveyed a warm smile and told the waitress thank you as she departed from the table with the dirty dishes that she had placed in a brown, medium sized, rubber, two handle grip tub.

After the waitress had left from our table, I looked directly at MERC and advised her to take a one and a half hour 'power nap' sitting up in the chair she was in and I would keep watch over her until she awoke. She agreed to the idea, closed her eyes and went to sleep as I sat on the chair I occupied awake as she rested.

While MERC slept in an upright position in the chair across the table from me, I poured in succession from the opened 750 ml bottle of 100 Proof (black label), Ruskova vodka, a half full glass every time I tilted it to my open mouth and guzzled half its contents as I silently reviewed in my head the Finalized Hit List, in order of priority. I rationalized if it was feasible or unfeasible to retain its arrangement in a particular order, which was influenced by the emphasis of those individuals' unaccountable for their repeated acts that were significant in the destruction of life, as follows:
- ONE GOVERNMENT's Chief Biomedical Engineer, Ivan Gott and recognized as a distinguished official of the regime. *His crimes committed are genocide/mass murder, unauthorized experimentation on human beings and sexual assault.*

MR. X - VIII

- ONE GOVERNMENT's Head of Artificial Intelligence (AI) Inventor Victor Young and recognized as an eminent official of the regime. *His crimes committed are contract killings, illegal organ harvesting/body parts snatching, identity theft, unauthorized creation of 'Semi-Human Clones' and sexual assault.*
- CRAZIED mob's leader, Manic's right-hand-man (second-in-command) named Schizo and praised with high esteem being the first living example of a human to be reborn as a CRAZIED from droplets of Manic's blood. *His crimes committed are homicide.*
- Vivian Young the twin sibling of Victor Young and devout representative of ONE GOVERNMENT. *Her crimes committed are collaborator and co-conspirator, exploitation, fraud, racketeering and sexual assault.*
- ONE GOVERNMENT Supreme, DEVIFETAN. *His crimes committed are eradication and extermination of the entire world's governments and everyone and everything related to them.*

I contemplated whether it would positively be beneficial to reconsider a change to the order, of the five remaining targets on the Finalized Hit List. I immediately considered which targets were the easiest targets with a practical 'in and out' advantageous rewarding kill ratio.

The Finalized Hit List was reprioritized only with the emphasis of advantageous rewarding kill ratio, in mind. These individuals' unaccountable repeated acts were forever significant and not to be ever overlooked of the destruction of life, they were accountable for, so the new version of it was, as followed:

- Vivian Young the twin sibling of Victor Young and devout representative of ONE GOVERNMENT. *Her crimes committed are collaborator and co-conspirator, exploitation, fraud, racketeering and sexual assault.*
- ONE GOVERNMENT's Head Artificial Intelligence (AI) Inventor Victor Young and recognized as an eminent official

MR. X - VIII

of the regime. *His crimes committed are contract killings, illegal organ harvesting/body parts snatching, identity theft, unauthorized creation of 'Semi-Human Clones' and sexual assault.*

- CRAZIED mob's leader, Manic's right-hand-man (second-in-command) named Schizo and praised with high esteem being the first living example of a human to be reborn as a CRAZIED from droplet of Manic's blood. *His crimes committed are homicide.*
- ONE GOVERNMENT's Chief Biomedical Engineer, Ivan Gott and recognized as a distinguished official of the regime. *His crimes committed are genocide/mass murder, unauthorized experimentation on human beings and sexual assault.*
- ONE GOVERNMENT Supreme, DEVIFETAN. *His crimes committed are eradication and extermination of the entire world's governments and everyone and everything related to them.*

MERC awoke exactly at the 1 ½ hour mark from the 'power nap' that she had taken seated in an upright position in the chair across the table from me. Shortly afterwards, she opened wide her large shiny black eyes, presented me with a big cordial smile and commented on how reinvigorated she felt having had the splendid opportunity to get some rest.

I smiled in return with an expression of amusement and asked her if she was ready to leave for the capital city of Moscow. MERC repeated the word Moscow with a degree of puzzlement within her tone of voice and facial appearance. I indicated to her that I would brief her as to the reason why we were to go there once the both of us had exited the nightclub, GALACTICA.

MERC and I stood up from the chairs we sat on around the table that was in the darkest far right corner section of the room closest to rear fire exit door, made our way through the crowd of people on the dance floor, headed toward the main entrance/exit of the nightclub and strolled outside. As soon as the both of us stepped into the outdoors and began to walk toward the

MR. X - VIII

road, MERC reminded me that it would be daylight in a little bit, over an hour's time. I concurred to her statement of concern with regard to daybreak materializing shortly and proposed that if we travelled on the shoulder of the M8 road with a 'sense of urgency' we should be able to reach the city of Chelyuskinskiy, 3.7 kilometres distance away, within 45 minutes just before sunrise, and rent a room for the day to rest and wash ourselves until evening before continuing on with our journey to the capital city of Moscow. MERC fully endorsed my recommendation by balancing on the balls of her feet inside the black Russian Army Sapogi (Jackboots) that she wore, to elongate her body, as she leaned herself against the left side of mine and erotically licked my left ear.

MERC and I entered the city of Chelyuskinskiy just before dawn and found a family owned and operated boarding house which had vacancies. MERC stepped inside the front foyer of the house that led to the lobby area and walked up to a little small-boned, silver longhaired elderly woman, who stood behind the reception desk. She inquired about any available rooms to rent for the day, as I waited outside for her and then without delay she handed over one polished oval black onyx gemstone to the polite elderly lady.

MERC, after having paid for a readily accessible room for us to use for the day, turned around and skipped with jubilation away from the reception desk, through the lobby, front foyer and outside the boarding house to where I vigilantly stood on the walkway for her to return. The both of us hastily walked together to the room, immediately unlocked the door to it with the room key that was given to her and promptly entered inside. As soon as we were inside the room, I instantly locked the door behind us, closed the curtains and switched on the wall mounted light that was attached at eye level between the closed door and chest of drawers positioned flush against the wall.

When MERC commenced to undress herself so she could get naked to take a hot bath, I then explained my reasons as to

M.R. X – VIII

why I reprioritized The Finalized Hit List, which would be favourable for us with expedient results to achieve our goal in assassinating the individuals marked as irreversible targets because of their unaccountable repeated acts significant to the destruction of life overall. She was in complete agreement with what I had advised her of in relation to the matter of the restructured Finalized Hit List.

While MERC fully immersed her slender, fit, curvy body in the Cast Iron Porcelain Claw foot Double Ended 1.70 metre long bathtub filled with hot water and soap bubbles that she lathered up her smooth orange colour skin and long curly gold hair with, I questioned her for significant information that would be worthwhile relating to Vivian Young and her twin brother Victor Young, ONE GOVERNMENT's Head Artificial Intelligence (AI) Inventor for when we took action to terminate their lives indefinitely after covertly infiltrating the fortified walls encircled around the capital city of Moscow, where they both lived.

MERC dunked her entire head underwater to rinse off the soapsuds that she had in her hair, emerged a moment later from beneath the water in the bathtub, wiped both her large shiny black eyes free of any soap bubbles on them and told me that Vivian Young and her twin brother Victor Young inhabited a permanent home together in the downtown area of the capital city of Moscow. She disclosed to me that they were given ownership of the historic Bolshoi Theatre located at Theatre Square 1, Moscow, Russia 125009 to do as they pleased. I commented that I knew precisely where the Bolshoi Theatre was positioned within the capital city of Moscow and quickly posed the question about what type of security system (manned or unmanned) was in place inside and outside building. MERC smirked and made a snide remark that Victor Young's security measures established, for his own personal safety, was a harem of attractive female, YES Cyborg Breeder Clones that accompanied him at all times while at home or away, except at night when asleep in

MR. X – VIII

the master bedroom with his twin sister Vivian Young. I slowly shook my head left to right a few times with revulsion to what MERC had told me in thought with the twins, Victor and Vivian Young. I commented to her if I was to assume that the both of them regularly committed incest together in a sexual relationship between two siblings. MERC affirmed it by actively nodding her head up and down. I could not help myself but to vent to her that having sexual intercourse with a sibling was surely 'down and dirty fucken sickening'.

MERC finished up with washing her entire body in the Cast Iron Porcelain Claw foot Double Ended 1.70 metre long bathtub as I exited the bathroom, to enter into the main room and vigilantly kept watch for any trouble should it appear at our doorstep. Approximately 15 minutes had gone by before MERC entered the main room from the bathroom, naked with a large white cotton tan stripe bath towel wrapped around her head of long curly gold hair. She fondly smiled at me, confirmed that the bathroom was open for me to use and that she drained all the dirty water in the bathtub, wiped it clean and refilled it with hot water for me to bathe myself. I thanked her for being thoughtful of me. I handed over to her, two MP-443 Grach, double-action, short-recoil semi-automatic pistols, then undressed naked and entered into the bathroom to take myself a hot bath. After I had washed myself clean, free of dirt and sweat on my body, I stepped out of the bathtub and emptied dirty water down the bathtub drain. I departed the bathroom and walked into the main room, where MERC lay on her left side on top of the king size bed, facing in the direction of the door and window, half naked with just a faded dark olive green Skinny Puppy industrial rock group, short sleeve t-shirt on with both MP-443 Grach, double-action, short-recoil semi-automatic pistols placed in front of her as she attentively listened for any unusual sounds outside.

I informed her that I would lie down beside her underneath the covers of the bed because I was in need of some sleep. I, was

MR. X - VIII

going to take a 3 hour 'power nap' and if she could please ensure to wake me within that timeframe. MERC turned her head toward me, sympathetically grinned and agreed to do so.

I was awoken from the 3 hour 'power nap' flabbergasted and speechless, to observe MERC overwhelmed with satisfaction as she repeatedly caressed, massaged, squeezed and stroked both my 'man-tool' and 'man-bag'. The purpose was intended to create a consistent steady flow of sperm out from the tip of the top segment of my 'man-tool', amassing every last spermicide until it had been depleted and drained by the 'Depletion Extraction Empty Process' (DEEP) to attain an accruement of quantity into her mouth and down her throat.

When MERC had completed DEEP, she licked her lips with her long thick pink tongue, looked up at me, grinned from ear to ear, reminded me that she was still a YES Cyborg Clone, originally created to provide a service of pleasure for sexual fulfilment to her once clientele and why not wake me, her boyfriend and lover from a 'power nap' by oral fulfilment.

I honestly confessed to MERC that what she had done to awaken me from the three hour 'power nap' was very refreshing erotically especially right before embarking on a mission that the both of us were to carry out to exterminate two individuals worthy of death for the despicable acts they had done to the innocent and naive.

I calculated that the trip on foot would be approximately 27.7 kilometres and take about 5 hours 31 minutes to reach the city of Moscow if we travelled on the E115 and the M8. MERC and I were both in agreement that we had to depart the rented room at the family owned and operated boarding house as soon as it became nightfall. At 19:55 hours we embarked on our journey under a sky of pitch black from the city of Chelyuskinskiy, route to the capital city of Moscow where the historic Bolshoi Theatre is located and Victor and Vivian Young could be found, together in one place at the same time to assassinate them.

ℳℛ. 𝒳 - VIII

At 00:25 hours MERC and I arrived undetected at the eastern section of the smoothly finished solid, impenetrable concrete wall, 9.1 metres thick x 21.3 metres high that encircled around the capital city. MERC gazed at me with a fixed unspoken show of discouragement pertaining to the obvious obstacle of the impenetrable concrete wall. I humorously smirked at her in silence and motioned for her to climb on to my back, grasp firmly both of my shoulders so I could give her another 'piggy back' ride, to creep us 'up-and-over' and down the wall, to the other side while effectively in a physiological colour change. Without hesitation MERC jumped on to my back, grasped firmly both of my shoulders for her 'piggy back' ride as I instantaneously implemented physiological colour change and slithered to the other side in a convincing artistry, totally oblivious to the ONE GOVERNMENT Soldiers around us on duty assigned to patrol on top the eastern area of the solid, impenetrable concrete wall, 9.1 metres thick x 21.3 metres.

Immediately after, MERC and I touched down on solid ground inside the capital city of Moscow, I turned my head to the left and whispered over my left shoulder for her to remain in the 'piggy back' position attached to my backside. I also instructed her to hold on tight, because it would be much quicker for us to get to the theatre, within several minutes, if I raced to it with her secure on my back, while in physiological colour change mode the entire time. She playfully bit down on my left earlobe, then licked the back portion of my neck as she rubbed chest and crotch in an up and down motion and quietly muttered to me to 'giddy-up'. We arrived outside the historic theatre within approximately 10 minutes, where the twin siblings, Victor and Vivian Young were settled in for the night.

All the while, currently in physiological colour change mode, MERC climbed down off of my back as I steadily held a continuous unbreakable grip around her right wrist with my right hand. Shortly after both of her feet were on the ground, I slightly loos-

MR. X - VIII

ened the grip of my right hand on her right wrist so she could replace it with her left hand without breaking the physiological colour change connection that was ongoing together with us.

MERC and I then advanced in a stealthy manner up the walkway to the front door of the premises, which was unlocked and we entered inside. Simultaneously, the both of us made our way through the building in the direction toward the master bedroom where Victor and Vivian Young lay asleep together. Just before we entered the hallway leading to the master bedroom, we came across Victor Young's personal security harem of attractive female, YES Cyborg Breeder Clones. These YES Cyborg Breeder Clones were preoccupied, engaged in V-VIPER, forcibly extracting every ounce of bodily fluid and semen from three former male employees of Victor Young that he had dismissed for their alleged incompetence as so-called creative ground-breaking innovators, earlier in the evening.

Whilst they suffered, paralyzed in severe agony and sheer terror on the gloss mahogany hardwood floor, MERC and I discretely walked past the group of YES Cyborg Breeder Clones and their three victims of entertainment. We soundlessly moved briskly down the hallway invisible to Victor Young's implemented type of security system, it manned by the use of YES Cyborg Breeder Clones that was utterly a joke to witness. Meanwhile we quietly opened the master bedroom door, noiselessly entered inside the bedroom and gently shut the door behind us, so as not to wake the twin siblings, who were asleep together in the traditional style, king size, blood red colour finish, sleigh wood constructed bed with genuine leather headboard or cause a distraction to interrupt the YES Cyborg Breeder Clones outside at the beginning point of the corridor into the hallway.

MERC and I carefully tiptoed with meticulous adjustments in our individual weight to the balls of our feet, so we could properly be in position to our respective assigned targets for rightful assassination. Victor Young lay naked, asleep flat on his back in

MR. X - VIII

the bed underneath the covers, which exposed himself from the waistline just below his bellybutton to top of his head. Vivian Young lay naked asleep on her right side with her back facing toward her twin brother, in the bed underneath the covers, that exposed her upper torso, with her left arm draped across her 100F size breast implants, which was one of the many routine cosmetic surgeries performed for her by her brother in an attempt to satisfy her addictive obsession, of achieving a final evolutionary phase of perfection in the attainment of flawlessness relating to a female human specimen. The instant we stood set, ready to execute, I looked directly over the incestuous twins, Victor and Vivian Young that have a regular ongoing sexual relationship together with one another, into MERC's large shiny black eyes. I winked as a cue to kill both of them simultaneously. MERC returned the look also directly over the incestuous twin siblings that were asleep naked together underneath the bed covers and winked back her approval guaranteed to my initial cue to terminate them at the same time.

MERC seized Vivian Young by the head. With her left hand, she tightly gripped the centre part of Vivian Young's forehead and her right hand firmly gripped her chin. Then with one powerful twist of force in a counter clockwise motion, MERC broke her neck and she died 'on-the-spot' with her eyes open.

I placed my left hand, palm down, over Victor Young's mouth and nose that prevented him from being able to breathe. I felt the bones in his face, begin to shatter and splinter into tiny pieces underneath his skin from the forceful restraint of pressure I continued apply to it. Then with the right middle finger on my right hand I transformed it into a miniature cylindrical pointed spear, approximately 33 centimetres in length that I deliberately inserted into Victor Young's left ear canal. It steadily pierced through his left ear drum, left external acoustic meatus, right external acoustic meatus, right ear drum and out of his right ear canal, all the while he underwent through unwavering agony that included being asphyxiated against his freewill before he died in shock.

MR. X - VIII

I withdrew the converted miniature cylindrical pointed spear that impaled Victor Young through the head and changed it back to my right middle finger on my right hand, to its normal appearance. I whispered to MERC that we effectively achieved our purpose here and it was now time to leave. She nodded in agreement to my recommendation, raised both hands to her mouth, puckered her lips together and blew a kiss in my direction.

The both of us, together, grasped with both our hands the ends of the purple top silk satin cover bed sheet and black bear shaggy genuine fur bedspread, pulled them over the deceased lifeless bodies of the twin siblings, Victor and Vivian Young, so as to not arouse the suspicion of someone, who would accidently enter their master bedroom unannounced.

Mr. X – VIII

Mr. X's Intimate Thoughts:

CAN YOU NOT SEE THE OBVIOUS?
THE ABANDONMENT AND DESERTION
OF HUMANITY
ESCALATING WITH CERTAINTY,
THOSE CONSIDERED USELESS

CAN YOU NOT SEE THE CONTRADICTIONS?
TO MEANINGFUL FULFILMENT AND
INHABITED WORTHWHILE
BECOMING INCREASINGLY IDLE,
FOR FUTILE PURPOSES

EMPTY CLUELESS SOULS
MUST SURELY KNOW
THAT CONTAINING NOTHING IN ITSELF
IS HOLLOW AND VOID

DO YOU NOT CARE TO INVESTIGATE?
THE INSENSIBLE DEALINGS UNORTHODOX
IN NATURE
CHALLENGING THE IMPORTANCE,
FOR MINDFUL AWARENESS

DO YOU NOT CARE TO UNDERSTAND?
THE CLEAR DANGERS THAT AWAIT YOU
THREATENING TO EMBARK, IN A REVOLUTION

MR. X - VIII

EMPTY CLUELESS SOULS
MUST SURELY KNOW
HAVING NO KNOWLEDGE IN ITSELF
IS HOLLOW AND VOID

ARE YOU NOT OVERCOME WITH NERVOUSNESS?
FROM THE MASTERFUL WROUGHT
OF EMBODIMENT
INSPIRING A TAKEOVER,
THROUGH ETERNAL GENOCIDE

ARE YOU NOT OVERCOME WITH EMOTION?
FOR THE MANY SO EASILY FORGOTTEN
REVEALING A FUTURE, INHERITED WITH HORROR

EMPTY CLUELESS SOULS
MUST SURELY KNOW
LACKING THE ESSENCE IN ITSELF
IS HOLLOW AND VOID

Momentarily afterward, MERC and I cunningly departed the master bedroom by leaving out through the stainless steel framed, antique decor glass inward-swinging windows, in physiological colour change mode unknown to anyone, who might be outdoors on the grounds of the property.

As soon as we were outside the historic, Bolshoi Theatre, home to Victor and Vivian Young and actively executing physiological colour change, we dashed together in unison using the exact route utilized earlier to gain access but in reverse to exit the capital city of Moscow, to return to the wasteland outside its smoothly finished solid impenetrable concrete wall, 9.1 metres thick x 21.3 metres high that encircled it entirely.

MR. X - VIII

DEATH DOES NOT DISCRIMINATE
IT ONLY ELIMINATES
DEATH DOES NOT DISCRIMINATE
IT ONLY TERMINATES
THOSE THAT ARE ABETTING

BOTH EYES OPEN
WILL NOW CLOSE

DEATH DOES NOT DISCRIMINATE
IT ONLY ELIMINATES
DEATH DOES NOT DISCRIMINATE
IT ONLY TERMINATES
THOSE THAT ARE BESETTING

A BEATING HEART
WILL NOW STOP

DEATH DOES NOT DISCRIMINATE
IT ONLY ELIMINATES
DEATH DOES NOT DISCRIMINATE
IT ONLY TERMINATES
THOSE THAT ARE CENSUSING

A BODY ALIVE
WILL NOW DIE

DEATH DOES NOT DISCRIMINATE
IT ONLY ELIMINATES
DEATH DOES NOT DISCRIMINATE
IT ONLY TERMINATES
THOSE THAT ARE SPECIALIZED
IN ADMINISTERING AGONY,
BETRAYAL AND CONFLICT

Conclusion

MR. X

❖ ❖ ❖

MERC and I continued to walk east into the wasteland away from the capital city of Moscow and its impenetrable concrete wall enclosure for approximately two hours before we arrived at a semi-ruined brick electrical utility building.

I gestured with my hands to MERC in silence that I would quietly check around the left side and for her to check the right side, and afterwards, we would link up behind the backside of the building. We both reached the back of the building about the same time and nodded to one another 'the all clear'. The both of us together without making a sound, quickly crept around to the front of the semi-ruined brick electrical utility building to ensure that it was possibly abandoned before we were to use it as a place to rest for the night.

Once MERC and I returned to the entrance of the building, I signalled to her to slowly slide open its dust covered thick metal black door as I stood ready at an offset angle away from the front of the door, but able to eliminate any possible threats that might be inside. With her right hand she gripped the D-shaped metal welded door handle and hastily slid the door open. I immediately used my thermal vision sensory to scan the entire medium size room from 'top-to-bottom' and found it to be empty.

We both looked at each other and smiled. MERC jokingly whispered in a flirtatious tone of voice, insisting that I enter into the room first. I declined in a gentlemanly manner and gestured with chivalry toward her that she go inside before me. She graciously smiled and seductively walked into the building as she alluringly shook her bum in front of me as I followed behind her.

MR. X

Afterwards, MERC and I settled into the temporary shelter until the next morning. I expressed my frustration with the difficulty and time it would take to close out The Finalized Hit List than I initially had expected with regards to:

- ONE GOVERNMENT's Chief Biomedical Engineer, Ivan Gott and recognized as a distinguished official of the regime. *His crimes committed are genocide/mass murder, unauthorized experimentation on human beings and sexual assault.*
- ONE GOVERNMENT Supreme, DEVIFETAN. *His crimes committed are eradication and extermination of the entire world's governments and everyone and everything related to them.*

I know realistically it would be outright suicide to attempt to terminate their existence without a fool-proof plan established, thorough preparation completed and adequate manpower obtained. But, the CRAZIED mob's leader, Manic's right-hand-man, Schizo was next on The Finalized Hit List to be executed and MERC and I would be coming for him soon without him ever knowing, that the бука (Buka), 'Boogie Man' never misses his target.

MR. X

MR. X's Intimate Closing Thoughts:

I WELCOME FULFILMENT OF HAPPINESS
BUT AM HUNTED BY MADNESS
AT THE SAME TIME

IT IS A WAR
CONTINUAL EACH AND EVERY DAY
BURNING INSIDE OF ME

I YEARN TO EXPERIENCE LAUGHTER
BUT AM SURROUNDED BY DISASTER
AT THE SAME TIME

IT IS A WAR
CONTINUAL EACH AND EVERY DAY
AS I WELCOME DEATH

I STRIVE TO LEARN CONTROL
BUT AM INVADED BY UNKNOWN
AT THE SAME TIME

IT IS A WAR
CONTINUAL EACH AND EVERY DAY
THAT INFLICTS ON ME PAIN

WAR WITHIN
I CAN-NOT BELIEVE
IT'S ME VERSUS ME

MR. X

MR. X's Intimate Closing Thoughts:

I WORK HARD
DAY IN AND DAY OUT
TO OVERCOME ANY PERSONAL DOUBTS
THROUGH BLOOD, SWEAT AND TEARS
BECAUSE I SEEK
HOPE FOR A NEW START

IT IS THE NATURE OF THE BUSINESS
IT IS THE SIGN OF THE BEAST

I HAVE RESPONSIBILITIES
TO MYSELF AND LOVED ONES
THAT CANNOT BE OVERLOOKED
THROUGH BLOOD, SWEAT AND TEARS
BECAUSE I KNOW
EXCUSES ARE FOR THE WEAK

IT IS THE NATURE OF THE BUSINESS
IT IS THE SIGN OF THE BEAST

I AM ACCOUNTABLE
FOR EVERYTHING THAT I DO
WHEN I HAVE TO CHOOSE
THROUGH BLOOD, SWEAT AND TEARS
BECAUSE I FEAR
THERE WILL BE NO TOMORROW

Mr. X

IT IS THE NATURE OF THE BUSINESS
IT IS THE SIGN OF THE BEAST

I MUST REALIZE
FOR THAT WHICH IS NEEDED
FOR ME TO FINALLY RECEIVE
THROUGH BLOOD, SWEAT AND TEARS
WHICH I REQUIRE
ANSWERS TO WHAT IS UNSPOKEN

IT IS THE NATURE OF THE BUSINESS
IT IS THE SIGN OF THE BEAST

MR. X

MR. X's Intimate Closing Thoughts:

THE BIG AND LITTLE HAND
ON EVERY CLOCK
SPIN ROUND AND ROUND
WITH EVERY TICK TOCK
ANTICIPATING TO SOUND

A NUMBER OF CLUELESS PEOPLE
GATHER INTO CROWDS
WITHOUT A REASON WHY
WITHIN EVERY CITY AND TOWN
ANTICIPATING TO DIE

DAYDREAMING
DAYDREAMING IN 3D
IS THIS FOR REAL
OR JUST MAKE BELIEVE?

CLOUDS FILL THE SKY
COLOURING IT BLACK
INTO ONE LARGE VOID
WITH EVERY LIGHTNING FLASH
AWAITING THE CHOSEN

Mr. X

ALL LIFE ON EARTH
WILL TRULY DIE
COUNTLESS IN ITS NUMBER
WITH EVERY ROLL OF THE DICE
ENVISAGING ONE AFTER ANOTHER

DAYDREAMING
DAYDREAMING IN 3D
IS THIS FOR REAL
OR JUST MAKE BELIEVE?

MR. X

MR. X's Intimate Closing Thoughts:

THEY SAY IT IS A VISION
BUT I KNOW
AND YOU CHOOSE NOT TO KNOW
THAT THIS IS SMOKE AND MIRRORS

MORNING, NOON AND NIGHT
THEY PROFESS THE TRUTH
TO THOSE OF STUPIDITY
WHO DESPERATELY NEED GUIDANCE

DELIRIOUS
IS WHAT THEY ARE
DELIRIOUS
THIS HAS GONE TOO FAR
JUST TO EARN A MARK

THEY SAY THEY HAVE NEW IDEAS
BUT I SEE
AND YOU CHOOSE NOT TO SEE
IT IS ALL NOTHING BUT LIES

MR. X

MORNING, NOON AND NIGHT
THEY PROFESS THE TRUTH
TO THOSE OF STUPIDITY
A PATHWAY TO ENLIGHTENMENT

DELIRIOUS
IS WHAT THEY ARE
DELIRIOUS
THIS HAS GONE TOO FAR
JUST TO EARN THEIR MARK

MR. X

MR. X's Intimate Closing Thoughts:

EVERY MORNING YOU WAKE
FROM THE OTHER DAY
THAT WAS SHADOWED IN MISFORTUNE

YOU MUST ASK YOURSELF
ARE YOU WASTING TIME
EXPECTING TO HIDE IN SILENCE

PASSING TIME
LIVING IN A LIE
PASSING TIME
LIVING IN A LIE

EVERY NIGHT YOU SLEEP
EXHAUSTED FROM THE DECEIT
OF THOSE FILLED WITH INDECENCY

YOU MUST ASK YOURSELF
ARE YOU WASTING TIME
ACCEPTING TO LIVE IN SILENCE

PASSING TIME
LIVING IN A LIE
PASSING TIME
LIVING IN A LIE

MR. X

MR. X's Intimate Closing Thoughts:

I TRAVEL ABROAD
MANY TIMES TIRED AND LOST
BUT I WILL SURVIVE
IN PURSUIT OF THE FUTURE

I AM ONE
ONE NOT OF SUSPICION

I AM THE EXTERMINATOR
FOR EVERY RECKLESS DECISION
BY THOSE NOT INNOCENT
UNWORTHY TO LIVE ANOTHER DAY

I AM ONE
ONE NOT OF SUSPICION

I AM ALIVE
FULL OF LIMITLESS LIFE
YOUR DAYS ARE FOREVER NUMBERED
JUST YOU WATCH AND SEE

Mr. X

I AM ONE
ONE COMMITTED TO JUDGEMENT

I AM THE GHOST
TERRORISM TO THE UNHOLY
AS THE FACELESS BOOGIE MAN
FOR WHICH I THRIVE

I AM ONE
ONE COMMITTED TO JUDGEMENT

novum PUBLISHER FOR NEW AUTHORS

Rate this book on our website!

www.novum-publishing.co.uk

The author

Novelist James K. Papay is an avid reader of all things sci-fi. In this, his debut novel, Mr. X: Assassin By Desire, Papay takes his sci fi into a whole newly created world.

Born in East Chicago, Indiana, Papay's move to Newcastle in the UK has allowed him to work within the security sector allowing some realism into his fantasy writing. Papay juggles his work and writing with family life including four children. His aim in his writing is to entice readers through his artistic imagination to experience the unexpected ...

novum 🔸 PUBLISHER FOR NEW AUTHORS

The publisher

> **He who stops being better stops being good.**

This is the motto of novum publishing, and our focus is on finding new manuscripts, publishing them and offering long-term support to the authors.
Our publishing house was founded in 1997, and since then it has become THE expert for new authors and has won numerous awards.

Our editorial team will peruse each manuscript within a few weeks free of charge and without obligation.

You will find more information about
novum publishing and our books on the internet:

www.novum-publishing.co.uk